CW01630745

Sunnyside Up

A collection of writings
by a group of delegates
from, and in support of

Swanwick
THE
writers'
SUMMER SCHOOL

This edition 2025

ISBN: 978-1-7396926-9-8

First published in 2025 by Amazon

Printed in the United Kingdom

Contents

Foreward

Writing is often seen a as solitary occupation and it can be if the writer sits alone in their attic with their notebook or even by themselves in a coffee shop in front of their screen. That is why writing groups, retreats and schools are so important to allow authors and poets to get feedback on their work, hone their skills and gather together to exchange views.

The authors in this anthology all met at The Writers' Summer School, which has been held at the Hayes Conference Centre every August since 1949. Since its inception, the school has been renowned for its friendly, nurturing spirit, and therefore it is no surprise that those who have enjoyed the company of other writers there should band together in an anthology in support of it, particularly when many of them met over breakfast at the school.

The authors and poets who shared their work in this book include Terry Baldock, who is well known for his competition-winning poetry and prose, and Sharon Cook, who has made the leap from professional journalist to bestselling author.

Also amongst the breakfast club are Maria Dorman and Bea Hutchings, both more known for poetry than prose, but who have included delightful short stories too and Shona Gilchrist, who writes well-crafted stories but surprised only herself when she also created excellent poetry.

Novelist Martin Lake has contributed stories that benefit from his sharp wit and good humour, and author and playwright Sue Noon delights with exquisite stories and a well-observed short play.

Last, but by no means least, the anthology goes international when the thought-provoking poetry of Irishman Liam Thompson completes the lineup.

My congratulations and respect go to all who worked so hard to produce this anthology. It is an inspirational book in support of an institution that brings writers together. The unity of purpose of the contributing writers refutes the claim that writing is a solitary occupation.

The Writers' Summer School was established to bring together those with a love of the written word and it is a delight to be able to read the fruits of the talents of eight of its most avid supporters.

Contributors:

Liam Thompson, Shona Gilchrist,
Maria Dorman, Sharon Cook,
Bea Hutchings, Sue Noon,
Terry Baldock, Martin Lake.

Terry Baldock

Terry is a short story and poetry writer who has been published in the United Kingdom and Hong Kong. He is a member of the Composers and Authors Society of Hong Kong (CASH).

He writes for competitions. Recently a winner in the Oldie poetry comp October 2023, Writing Magazine unreliable narrator July 23, 2nd in Writing Magazine's 'Back to the Eighties' October 2023, winner Swanwick Writers Summer School poetry competition July 2024, runner up in Spellbound/Val Penny short story competition July 2024, poem in the King Lear Anthology 2024 and a poem in The Daily Mail in December 2024.

Leave It To Tomorrow

By Terry Baldock

(Winner Writing Magazine Spotlight Competition Nov 23)

There's a 'new' Beatles record. A John Lennon recording that's been Artificially Intelligenced. I've always been a fan. As has most of the world.

I used to collect vinyl. Asia was a great place to find obscure collectibles. Late eighties and I was in a dusty, sweltering record shop in Djakarta, sifting through racks of discs. When the roar of a Harley Davidson motorbike stopped outside. A figure walked in. It must have been a hundred degrees, but this guy was in full leathers. He took off his helmet. 'Ave you got any Uriah Heep albums?' he asked with, what I assumed, was a Dutch accent. A strange question in a strange place.

'No. Sorry. No Heep,' the proprietor replied.

The rider nodded his thanks and looked at me in a conspiratorial way. 'You a collector?'

I nodded through beads of sweat. 'Beatles,' I said.

'Contact me.' He handed me a card. Turned, left the shop, and roared away; someone chanting, replaced the motorcycles' anachronistic snarl.

'Call to prayer,' the shop owner started to usher me towards the door.

I looked back at the racks of unsorted vinyl.

'You go!'

The heat hit me. I looked at the card with what I assumed was the rider's details and made my way back to the hotel which, luckily, wasn't too far. The air conditioning hit me like a lover, welcoming me home. Shower, clean clothes, a cold drink, and I was ready.

I telephoned the number on the card.

'Hello. Dolph speaking.'

'The motorbike guy?'

'You the Beatles fan?'

'Yes.'

'I got something may interest you.'

'What is it? Indonesian pressings of albums, pirate copies?'

'Much better than that. An unknown recording. Where you staying?'

I told him. Within the hour I was standing in a plush apartment.

I'd been assured by the hotel staff that Mr Dolph was trustworthy, he frequented the hotel, and there couldn't be two like him.

'Unknown recording,' he said.

'From where?'

'Hong Kong. They played there in 1964. Must have been bored so they noodled around in the hotel.'

'And this is the noodling?'

'Yes. Only three quarters of a noodle. Jimmy Nichol was standing in for Ringo.'

'I remember.'

Then the unmistakable sound of the Beatles enraptured the room. An unknown song; a heartrendingly beautiful ballad.

'Beatles? Yes?'

'Sounds like it. Must be worth a lot of money. Is that the only copy?'

Dolph nodded. 'Not mine. Belongs to a friend. I take you to see him. Pick you up at eight.'

I said I couldn't wait. But I had to. He never showed up.

Next morning the guy behind the desk showed me an English language newspaper and there on the front page was Dolph. He'd been killed. Mugged.

That song died with him. It has never been released. Could be out there somewhere; someone may have it and doesn't know. It could turn up in the future. I'll leave it to tomorrow, but, as John Lennon said, tomorrow never knows.

Dead Ahead

By Terry Baldock

(Second – Esther Chilton - 250 word short story Sep 24)

What would you do If you came across a coffin in the middle of the road on a cold dark night? A dark rectangle against snow. Unknown against known.

They had.

It was as If It had risen from hell.

George slammed on the brakes.

'What on earth!'

'Or not,' Penny giggled, fourth glass of wine was taking effect.

'Or not what?'

'Of this earth.' She shook her head. 'It's a coffin.'

George nodded.

'In the road.'

He nodded again.

'What are we going to do?'

George thought. 'Could have fallen off the back of a hearse.'

'A second-hand coffin. Shall we have a look.' Penny made to open the door. Then screamed.

'What was that for?'

'I saw it move. Call the police. They'll know what to do.'

Creatures of the night were beginning to take an interest in the car's headlights.

They'd soon get a whiff of the couple and start biting, that's what George thought.

'Let's just go.'

'What if another car crashes into it?'

The coffin lid moved. A hand appeared. A naked man rose from within.

He looked at the frozen couple then at his surroundings.

'What the hell,' he groaned. 'It's me stag do. I was expecting a stripper. He waved his hands. Help!' Then noticed that he was naked.

The words lost in the dust and insects as the car roared away.

What would you do if you came across a coffin in the middle of the road on a dark night?

The Toolbox

By Terry Baldock

(Winner Writers Forum Poetry July 2018)

I found my Dad's toolbox
The other day,
Dumped in the garage.
Hidden away.

A fold out lid
That held old screws,
Tools inside that he'll
Never use.

There's hammers and spanners
And bits for drills.
Old Polyfilla
That no longer fills.

Screws to put in and
Screws taken out,
Picture hooks, wire and
Pieces of grout.

Packets of nails that
He never used.
All forgotten when
He was confused.

The saw that created
My cricket stumps.
The train he made me,
When I had mumps.

He wasn't a carpenter,
Or joiner by trade,
But we were so proud of
Things that he made.

Tables, lamps, wardrobes
And shelves.
Things that we couldn't have
Made for ourselves.

All being sold except
Loved souvenirs,
That have meant something
Over the years.

Things put together,
Things taken apart.
How can an old box
Break someone's heart?

Luggage

By Terry Baldock

(Originally published in the The Oldie October 2023)

They were the Windrush generation.
Smart suits, shoes, ties, and hats.
Looking more like bureaucrats.
Anxious smiles, expectant faces.
Carrying small suitcases.

Much needed talents, useful skills.
Welcome hugs, open arms.
Then work in factories, or on farms.
Arriving here from far flung places.
Carrying small suitcases.

Some with excellent qualifications,
Given jobs on buses or trains.
Barely enough to tax their brains.
Worried about how they'd cope.
Carrying small suitcases
Filled with hope.

Doronophobia (The Fear of Gifts)

By Terry Baldock

(Originally published in the Daily Mail 18th December 2024)

They're there under the tree!
And…and…there's some for me!
I know I should dance with glee,
But presents scare the hell out of me.
What if I don't like what's inside?
Quietly slip away and hide,
What should I do?
I'll feel like screaming but say thank you.
And what if they don't like what I've bought?
I panicked not giving a thought.
I feel like running, hiding, covering my eyes,
I'm worried it won't be a lovely surprise,
Their faces will be smiling but not their eyes.
Oh, I hate it with a vengeance.
Every Christmas a sad remembrance.
And those songs drive me crazy,
The suffering staff really amaze me.
I run screaming from shops playing Mariah Carey,
So, I have to be very wary.
And there's Paul McCartney's Wonderful Christmas time,
Give me some rap, a bit of grime.

And Slade's Merry Christmas Everybody,
I drop my shopping, leave the trolley.

It starts in August
To optimise the profit,
But surely there is really only one prophet.
Please! Please! Please! Stop it!
There may be presents, a cornucopia,
But I suffer from doronophobia.
As long as it's not metrophobia for me,
Because that's a fear of poetry.

Uh-Huh

By Terry Baldock

(Winner Swanwick Writers Summer School Poetry Competition 2024)

I used to be an Elvis Impersonator.
Late Elvis, not Hound Dog.
And I'd get booked for parties,
The suit, the wig, the whole hog.
With a couple of guys on guitar and drums,
No karaoke for me,
Then someone booked me for a Diamond Jubilee.

I used to be an Elvis Impersonator.
Curled lips, shaking hips, the works.
And I got booked for this party,
By a bunch of drunken jerks.
When I sang the song 'Too Much',
Some woman grabbed my crutch with glee,
Why did someone book me for a Diamond Jubilee.

I used to be an Elvis Impersonator.
So good I made women scream.
They'd throw their undies on the stage,
Like a wide-awake bad dream.
I'd chuck them scarves wet with sweat

As they screamed for bits of me,
Why did someone book me for a Diamond Jubilee.

I used to be an Elvis Impersonator.
They knew I wasn't real.
But arms reached out to grab me,
Trying to cop a feel.
I should have got danger money,
A bodyguard or three.
Why ever did they book me for a Diamond Jubilee.

I used to be an Elvis Impersonator.
A man of tunes with words.
And I got booked for a party,
Full of nouns, adjectives, and verbs.
I thought that they were writers,
Got knocked out during performance po – e – tree,
Never impersonate Elvis at a Swanwick Writers Jubilee.

The Cartographer

By Terry Baldock

(Originally published in King Lear Anthology 2024)

He was a map maker.

Walking the country with compasses, drawing materials, tape measures;

Recording everyday things and treasures.

Castles, schools, post offices, and junctions;

Ballrooms, village halls, places for functions;

Railways, embankments and cuttings shown as tadpoles;

Bridges, tunnels, huge quarried holes;

Sand, lakes, streams, rivers and locks;

High and low water, brooks, harbours and docks;

Cliffs, caves, contours, loxodromes;

Churches, chapels, cemeteries, old people's homes;

Woods, forests, trees and holy places;

Pitches and huge stadiums to hold races;

Escarpments, bridges, tunnels, mills, both wind and water;

Crossed swords showing battlefields as places of slaughter;

Hamlets, towns, settlements and villages;

Names of every place, Saxon or Norman pillages.

Boundaries, fences, bench marks, heights;

Places of recreation and other delights;

Abbeys, palaces and old priories;
Libraries for tourists to make enquiries;
Lanes, avenues, dotted bridle ways,

Where wagons once were hauled by drays.
His plans showed every shop, bank and hall,
But where one place should have been, there was nothing at all.
The error was noticed many years later,
When his maps were valued as much as Mercator.
He used scales like an inch to a mile,
But there was no standard to measure her smile.
She gave back his ring, weary of his wandering,
He, unaware, of the love he was squandering.
Only one place shows no house, path, or garden;
His heart, once soft, had started to harden.
He removed her house from every map,
They all showed nothing, just a big gap.
Now it's seen easily from high up above,
The old charts just say -
'Here Lie the Ruins of a Mapmaker's Love'.

Nobody Laughed

By Terry Baldock

(Originally published in Writing Magazine 2nd 1st person comp October 2022)

I died on stage that night. Not a heart attack, sniper's bullet, jealous husband. No, it was a bad joke, no boom boom moment jokewise, but it felt like an arrow in my heart. Can't afford an audience that doesn't laugh. And they booed as I left the stage. I'd not been booed since we first started all those years ago. Ronnie and Rex. That was us. Not the other way round. We stood with me on the left facing the crowd, Rex on the right, and that was forever. It couldn't be varied, didn't work. I had a space next to Rex, and he next to me. That was it. Until he died. I mean really died. Then that space where he should have been; had been for three decades, was empty.

'Change careers,' Bill, my manager said, after I came off. 'Or look for a new partner. You're just not funny anymore.'

'That means I was funny once. Eh Bill?'

'Not on your own you weren't. And the material was better. Punchy. Relevant. Not rude like now. No politics. Pity you fell out with Gordon. His stuff was perfect for your act.'

'Yeah, but he's moved on to bigger things. I was the comedian in the duo, Rex was the straight man, fed me the lines, took all the mock insults.'

'He was. But without him you've nobody to insult. Unless you do it to yourself.' He laughed.

'Do I have to do the second show tonight Bill? I'm not feeling too good.'

'Cost you a lot if you don't. Breach of contract. Have to pay. I mean you're here, aren't you? Go on. Do your best.

Imagine that Rex was there by your left arm. Take some medicine or something. I mean if you're feeling a bit funny that's just what you want.' He chuckled.

I always imagined that Rex was there. That was the trouble. The ghost of him. And ghosts aren't funny. No fun in the afterlife, I thought, couldn't be much fun being dead.

I went on as Bill suggested. Could see the first ten rows. Grim looking bunch. I tried an opening witticism. But they didn't want that. This lot had come along to see the legendary Ronnie Cox, half of the Ronnie and Rex duo, so as there was only half of the team there, maybe I'd be at least half as funny, I could see it in their faces, but I wasn't. And they hadn't paid half price.

'I thought the other half of the act was dead. Not you,' someone shouted, and others laughed. It was a bigger laugh than I managed to get.

I grinned. Tried to calm them down.

'Leave him alone,' a woman in a comedy hat shouted in my defence.

I nodded my thanks.

The spotlights dimmed. It went quiet. Time seemed to slow. Except it didn't affect me. Dust circled, tried to form a shape. I froze. 'Tell them about us,' a voice I barely recognised whispered from the vortex. 'Tell them our tale. That's what they want. Our story.'

It was Rex. The dust, the chill, the love he had for me, for the act, for each other. But he was deceased. No longer with us. And yet he whirled there, taking a Rex like form, wearing the hat, the suit, the tie that was so loud you could hear him coming. That was what he had said many times, and it was.

He faded. The lights rose, audience started to applaud, my left arm jerked as if something had let go.

They rose in unison. But why? How? Rex wasn't really there was he? I'd been to his funeral. Read the eulogy. Kissed his widow, Emily. That was it. I'd felt anger emanating from his casket as she cried on my shoulder. His kids consoling us.

TV cameras, reporters, words shouted, silly questions, 'What are you going to do now Ronnie?' 'You carrying on?'

'Mr Cox has not made a decision yet.' 'He's lost a great friend and colleague.'

We struggled to the car. Molly and Emily and Rex's two eldest kids.

'How do you feel about your partners death?' That was the last question thrown.

How was I supposed to feel. After all, I'd killed him.

'No comment,' Patricia our agent said, and the car whisked us away to the quiet wake. Only a select few. No hangers on. No fans.

'Suspicious Death', was what some of the early editions had said after Rex had been found. 'Misadventure' was another reason bandied about. Whatever that is. An adventure that went wrong. Or one that had been poorly chosen. Either would explain what had happened. It was me that chose it.

I remember having him up against the wall, arm at his throat. We'd often lost our tempers. Living cheek by jowl is hard. We shared much of each other's waking moments, rehearsals, travelling, late nights, too much drink, crooked theatre owners, filthy lodgings; then the good times, with awards, accolades, we were the best, most popular, the people's choice. Until I fell for his wife, and she fell for me, and secrets are hard to keep when you live in the same pocket, share the same breaths, rely on jokes, being funny, bouncing off each other like rubber twins. Brothers who hated each other. Caine and Abel. It was all going so well until I killed him.

Didn't mean to. Anger boiled over. Rex wasn't the fittest of men, and I knew this. But I went on. Pushed harder until his head almost exploded. I let go as he fell to the floor. The dressing room seemed to be a fitting place for a comedian to die. Misadventure was the cause although how my arm across his throat could have been deemed to be that, was hard to see, but then a good lawyer can make anything believable. I had a good lawyer. Anyway, I'd been with my wife at the time, hadn't I? She said I had.

I'd first met Molly when Rex and I were just about to give up. Lowest ebb. We blamed the audience for not having a sense of humour, or the town where we were playing for being miserable and humourless, which they were, but we were supposed to make them happy, give them a reason to go back home, go to work with a smile. We didn't.

But then it was a dull world until we met Gordon Robins who was a juggler cum ventriloquist, who was a frustrated comedy writer. He gave us some material, 'gave' us for goodness' sake, later he charged a lot, but we got laughs from it. Back then laughs were currency on the circuit.

Our reputation grew and we had an agent, a manager, and everything that comes with success. Radio and then television. Radio was an opening, but it was guesting on television that did it. Showed the world what we looked like, where we stood, me left him right. Me tall and slightly balding, him a bit chubbier with a sweeter more trustworthy face. The women loved him, though I got the biggest laughs.

A laugh is like a sleeping animal, prod it and it will wake and power its way into the ether, untamed, unstoppable. We prodded lots, set many free. Some died or faded, others took on lives of their own. We had conquered the comedy world and it was ours to lose. And we lost it.

Firstly, with Gordon leaving us. Then marital infidelity. And me killing Rex.

But he was there with me on stage. Feeding me the lines from our old shows. Beyond the grave comedy and this audience couldn't stop laughing and shouting. Rex wasn't there, only I could see and hear his ghost, or so I thought.

The audience could as well.

The spotlight picked out something next to me that looked a bit chubby, the clothes shimmered, his hat from our early days perched on his head, too small, very comedic.

I staggered off to the applause, something that I hadn't heard for a while, but were they applauding a ghost, the afterlife of Ronnie and Rex.

Bill opened the dressing room door for me. 'Brilliant. Absolutely brilliant.'

'Congratulations, Ronnie, terrific set.' One of the backstage staff said. And others gave me the thumbs up.

I tried to bathe in their praise, but Rex had always joked that you could get burnt if you bathed in it for too long. Jut a brief dip would be OK, for Rex's sake.

'How did you do it?'

'I didn't want to let Rex down, his memory, so I did stuff from our old acts. He was there beside me. I could feel him.' I took off my 'Ronnie' jacket.

'It was as if he was there, Ron.' Emily appeared at the door. 'Like old times.'

I wondered if she thought that it was a good thing that Rex had stepped back through the curtain of death, she was his widow after all. Our affair had stopped after Rex's passing, although 'passing' didn't seem to be the appropriate word.

'Ronnie and Rex are Back!' said a headline in a review of our act in the local weekly paper. The nationals wanted an interview. Bill thought it was a good idea. I went on a local television news programme, 'Just for a chat', they said.

I sat on a sofa.

'Shouldn't you be at the other end?' the interviewer joked. 'The way you always were on stage.'

I did as asked, to much merriment and applause.

The audience gasped. The monitors showed me on the sofa but on the other side there was a shape forming, it was Rex. In his pomp. Looking the way he always had. But he wasn't on the sofa, only on the monitor.

The interviewer didn't notice. 'Tell me Ronnie. If Rex was here now, what would you say to him?'

'But he isn't. I think that's an inappropriate question.'

The mist started to form again, cold, menacing, no longer friendly. 'Ask him why he killed me!' It shouted. 'Or is that inappropriate!'

Nobody laughed.

Sharon Cook

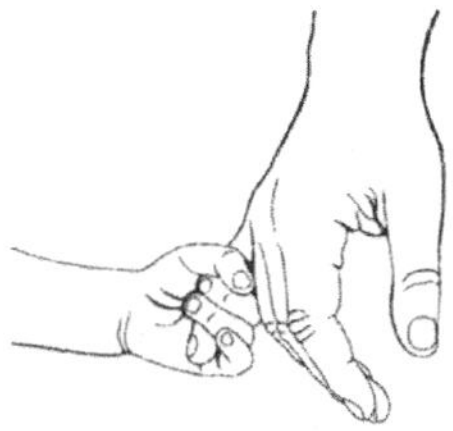

Sharon Cook is a former news journalist who now writes books. Last year 'Sewing Sequins on My Straight Jacket' was indie published: it went straight to number one, and has remained in the Amazon best seller charts ever since. Not too shabby for a (funny) memoir about childhood cancer… The reviews have made the author cry, and laugh!

Sharon skidded to a halt in the West Country some years ago, with two young children in tow, (yes, her own) who have since morphed into young adults. They've had quite a few adventures, some more fulfilling than others, but have always, eventually, been able to return to their seventeenth century stone cottage.

One day Sharon plans to write novels full time, rather than working in prison libraries, running creative workshops or perfecting the art of rejection by literary agents. Collecting vintage and coaxing her camper van out of its parking spot keep Sharon out of trouble – mostly. In times of deep stress, she makes chutney and fruit liqueurs. The cupboards are often full. The rest of the time she can be found hanging around literary festivals, or working with a blue light charity, where inspiring people and stories are never far away.

Chicken Feet - Best Served Cold

By Sharon Cook

She took off her conical hat, the chin strap of pink flowered fabric folded neatly inside. She placed it on the back shelf of the coach.

Isn't it the naughty ones who sit at the back? She looked the same as all the other old women. Until I spotted what was in the clear plastic bag, nestling under her bamboo hat. Chicken claws. Fresh. Congealed blood smeared the sweating plastic.

I imagined her running around the green leafed village we'd just driven through – dust covered cafes serving coffee, Fanta and bowls of pho – chopping off all the chicken feet in the village. When there were no chickens left to butcher, she ran straight to the coach, and now she's hiding at the back, next to me.

I know her naughtiness; her brown eyes are twinkling and she's looking at me. No, she's staring.

'Bracelet. I give you bracelet,' she said.

I smile. She smiles.

She knows I'm naughty. I know she's a survivor, her wrinkles silent testimony. A five-hour coach ride to Ho Chi Min City just got interesting.

Out of her cavernous shoulder bag, roughly stitched from an old rice sack, quite de rigour round here, she produces another plastic bag, much smaller than the one now resting behind our heads. It's stuffed with brightly coloured beads, fabric scraps, gaudy plastic combs and miniature fans. She rummages, the wrinkles around her eyes on overtime.

With a look of triumph, she fishes out a length of beads threaded onto a bright blue strip of material. Before I can take evasive action, she has tied it round my left wrist. I am staggered, not by the swiftness of her move, but by the bracelet. It is a surprise, its white glass beads, some shot through with silver and green, echo a necklace of my grandmother. Despite its beauty I am reluctant to buy it; I don't want to give her the wrong message, that I'm a white American with guilt money to throw around. And I don't want to spend the journey fobbing her off, have to move to a less appealing seat to escape her attentions.

'Is OK,' and she smiles at me again. 'I know you not real tourist. You too interested in my country. I think you writer man.' And she laughs at the expression on my face.

'And you, bracelet lady, are no ordinary bus traveller, are you?'

She nods her head, rummages in her bag, pulls out a large bottle of water. It's not been long out of a fridge, the condensation a testimony to its coolness. I am compelled to drink from my own bottle, even though it's warm.

'You need coconut water. Next stop. I get you coconut, full of good things, good for sweating, help cool.' I know she is laughing at me, but her smile is infectious. 'Bracelet is your present. I not want your money.' She is also a mind reader.

'Thank you for the bracelet. Did you make it?'

'No. Not my craft,' she said, barely taking her eyes off my face. 'I make other things. Important make people happy. Happy good. I think you happy, why I give you bracelet. You have good smile, Buddha like you, he like your smile.'

The bus is almost full, it's a holiday weekend and many Vietnamese are heading back to family in Ho Chi Min City. The tourists look hot and sweaty.

'Do you live in Ho Chi Min?'

'Saigon,' she said, looking furtively around her. 'Always Saigon. I live many places, I work Saigon. I am teacher.'

I was surprised, she looked, well, old. But maybe no one retires here. Everywhere I've seen people older than my grandmother working in restaurants, sweeping streets, in the markets, particularly in the markets, where 100-year old eggs could have been named after so many of the stall holders.

'You surprise I work,' and she laughed again. 'I see what you think in your eyes, you have open face.'

I could bottle this woman.

'I teach you cook. You come my nephew restaurant in Saigon and I teach you cook, then I teach you how eat. Our food good. We make fish sauce; nuoc mam make food happy.'

I had fallen in love with Vietnamese cuisine, it was true fusion food, not cheffed-up platefuls of invention. Roadside cafés and street stalls served as good as the restaurants, and even if I didn't always know what I ate, nothing so delicious could be bad, could it?

'So you teach cooking?'

'Sometimes cooking. One day my kitchen God, Tao Quan, say Li, teach people how cook. Always listen to God who has round belly and smiling face. I learn from my mother. She make food from nothing.'

At the next stop Li dived off the coach, leaving her bags behind, and returned minutes later with two large, hairy green coconuts, a hole hacked off the top and a bright purple, plastic straw sticking out of each one. The mellow juice danced with my taste buds. It was a cooling liquor which even seemed to slow my pulse, made me smile. I saw no stall selling them and no one else on the coach had one.

'Plant electric,' she said, laughing at her own joke.

I'd read about the electrolytes, the food scene was abuzz with everything coconut from its juice to its oil and flesh ground to flour. I'd be buying into the coconut scene when I got home.

By the time we reached the outskirts of Ho Chi Min City I had agreed to meet Li at her nephew's restaurant the following day, to have a cookery lesson, then lunch. She wrote it all down in my notebook.

'Opposite Ben Thanh, prime spot, made of pallets. Taxi drivers know. I take you Ben Thanh night market, shopping, you like, yes! I teach you make 'pho', you never be hungry in life with good pho.'

She got off the coach before the Backpackers District, where my hotel was booked. 'Hey, Li, don't forget your other bag,' I said, as she stood to go. I got the familiar smile, the chicken claws looked rancid.

'Is Ok, my nephew restaurant is vegetable.' She disappeared down a dusty side street, criss-crossed with so many overhead wires you could barely see sky.

I felt like a grinning god after a hot shower and a bowl of exceptional beef and potato curry, washed down by iced Saigon beer. I slept for hours, despite the Reunification fireworks and partying of locals mingling with travellers. My magazine editor was going to be pleased. Not only was he getting an under-budget travelogue on the land of the 'Rising Dragon', the place I had yearned to see since birth, he was also getting a food feature, the kind I knew our readers craved. Must get some decent photos tomorrow…

Seeking out a banh mi for breakfast, a better baguette than I've managed from many a French boulangerie, it was stuffed with pate and fresh pickled vegetables so good I wanted another immediately. I marvelled at a country which had embraced so much food heritage from its Chinese and French occupiers, turning brutality into glory, merging sweet and sour, while shunning the travesty known as 'hotdog'. My head was full of it, I had to get some of this down on paper and I was looking forward to meeting Li again.

I hailed a taxi, agreed a price in many millions of dong, in my world a couple of dollars, and was soon dropped outside a wooden edifice draped in plants and thousands of white fairy lights. As I climbed the rough wooden steps Li greeted me, her face a picture of benign happiness, her twinkle undimmed.

'My nephew want meet you,' she said, beckoning me through tables and benches that looked like they'd been made at a day workshop for the uninterested. 'He in kitchen.'

The 'kitchen' was shed-like, basic utensils hung off suspended broom handles and stock pots were simmering on an encrusted range cooker, wooden worktops piled high with chopped vegetables and fresh herbs, most of which I couldn't identify, towers of well-used woks wobbled by two glassless windows. A breeze wafted smells around. My mouth watered.

A man tall for this country, who looked my age, finished chopping the last of a sack of onions, his knife skills bordering on super human. He turned, his brown eyes looked me up and down before he wiped his hands on a stained calico apron tied round his child-like frame, a slow smile lighting up his face.

‘So you her yesterday bus traveller,’ and he laughed, nodded. ‘American, yes?’

I nodded. He held out his hand, a hand which seemed strangely familiar. ‘I pleased meet you Mr Cliff. I Li nephew, Bao.’ He laughed. ‘I make you coffee, Li come back soon.’ I hadn’t even seen her go.

We sat, on a balcony out the back, overlooking several filthy back alleys, scrawny cats marauding round every shadow. Coffee dripped through metal filters sat on white coffee cups, an open tin of condensed milk, with a teaspoon in the middle, sat on the table. Trails of incense scented the air. Coins, fruit and full coffee cups further offerings on the ornate alter by the kitchen doorway. Red silk flags hung from the ceiling.

‘You really not know who my auntie is?’ and he looked me in the eye, silence hung between us as if a silk lantern in a back alley.

I shook my head, slightly puzzled.

‘I believe in what you say.’ He drank some of his coffee. ‘My auntie,’ and he laughed, a deep belly laugh. ‘My auntie was Vietcong leader, big leader. Feared leader. She saved many lives. She killed many men. And you know what she do, when she find old enemy of Vietcong?’

I shook my head, only now beginning to realise how much the bracelet could cost me.

‘She go to their village. She chop feet off all their chickens. Then she make soup. Yesterday,’ he said, ‘our auntie made soup.’

Holding Hands

By Sharon Cook

(Manor House Writers 28/3/17)

I didn't get to be the first
To hold my son's hand
Or my daughter's.
Flat on my back
In a theatre with no stage
A blue-coated nurse
Claimed the privilege
The surgeon
Busy Stitching.
I think it's why,
Today,
I take the chance
To hold their hands
Whenever I can.

Slicing Lemons

By Sharon Cook

Think about sisters.
Relish time
Use fresh Thyme
In cooking.
Agree with the values
Of Others.
Stick with your own kind
Find your own kind
Use your own mind
Pick flowers
Wander gardens.
Hear voices,
Be selfish
Be selfless.
But do stop,
Speak out
Hear People.
Be able to sit
And find reasons
To slice lemons
Into drinks.

She Flies ...

By Sharon Cook

She flies at night. All the stories speak of dark corners and cold crevices. But it's not always true, oh no! I've seen her, flying clittered Dartmoor rocks, hunting for lost children to steal away. She feeds on fear, spiders, gorse prickles and abandoned picnics.

People run from her when the mists thicken and they are only thick, in daylight. Hairy Hands and Whist Wolves pale at the sight of the Running Hare ...

I know she doesn't always hunt at night. She's my mother now, and she won't let me go out, whatever the time of night, or day.

The Fight of Her Life

By Sharon Cook

Fighting her way through clod after clod, pushing back rotted leaves and needle-sharp thorns she made it to the surface, the tiniest shoot of green forged through ice hard soil.

Almost seeing sky, she pushed further and, to the glory of all around, she saw blue skies, the warmth of light after dark. It made her roots want to dance and never stop swaying in the breeze of promised head-bobbing splendour, a shared magnificence of the joyful carpet, a nod to spring on the bleak horizons of a New Year.

A cheer went up from all those around, snowdrops everywhere.

Maria Dorman

Born, bred, and educated in Kent, Maria waited until she retired to graduate. A lifelong avid reader and occasional dabbler in the written word, she discovered a love of writing in 2004. Upon retirement in 2015, Maria began a Master's degree in Creative Writing at Anglia Ruskin University, Cambridge, which led to her first visit to Swanwick in 2016.

Maria's genre of choice for writing is cosy crime, but she enjoys having a go at anything, so long as the word count is low! Married with three adult daughters and five grandchildren, she is now embarking on writing with her ten year old grandson. And maybe finishing her novella…

Just Think

By Maria Dorman

(This poem is my first attempt at a Pantoum, and was great fun to write. I found, however, that it needed 'topping and tailing' or it might have gone on and on!)

You ask me why you should eat well.

So heed my words as this tale I tell...

When you were small
I gave you milk.

You'd take it all,
You'd drink and drink.

I gave you milk,
I fed you food.

You'd drink and drink
And all was good.

I fed you food,
You ate and ate.

And all was good,
You put on weight.

You ate and ate.
I thought you'd pop!

You put on weight,
But you wouldn't stop.

I thought you'd pop!
I fed you less.

But you wouldn't stop,
You were such a mess.

I fed you less,
It was too late.

You were such a mess
With so much weight.

It was too late.
You couldn't stop.

With so much weight.
You just went pop.

When you were small, I fed you milk.

You'd take it all – why didn't I think?

Dear John

By Maria Dorman

(This poem was written in 2022 at Swanwick after a distressing phone call with my uncle who was suffering from dementia. It was read at his funeral.)

When the days stretch ahead and time seems all awry,
And they put you to bed but you can't fathom why
It's all wrong
Know this…
You are precious
you are loved
you are missed

When your love is long gone and you're lonely as hell
But you try to hang on to the moments that tell
Of your life
Know this:
You are precious
you are loved
you are missed

When you're lost in the mist and forget what is real;
And you want to get pissed but are given a meal
You don't like
Know this:
You are precious
you are loved
you are missed

We will weep for your pain as you struggle to cope,
Try again and again to show how we hope
You know this:
You are precious
you are loved

you are missed
WE LOVE YOU

Viral Tap, Volume Eleven

By Maria Dorman

(This poem was written as part of a creative writing course which was subsequently cancelled halfway due to the second Covid-19 lockdown!)

Slogans here, slogans there,
Feel the fear everywhere.
Tell me why I should care.

Stay at home, save a life.
If you must, leave the
☐ fife ☐ knife ☐ strife ☐ wife*

Hands-face-space, such disgrace
Dare you now show your face,
Or ignore track and trace?

Stay at home, save a life.
If you must, leave the
☐ fife ☐ knife ☐ strife ☐ wife*

New lockdown makes you frown.
Sit at home, watch The Crown
Till the R rate comes down.

Stay at home, save a life.
If you must, leave the
☐ fife ☐ knife ☐ strife ☐ wife*

*Choose in line with local lockdown procedures

The Missing Epiphany

By Maria Dorman

(A friend who teaches English to adults gave me a list of sixteen rarely used words from which I created this mini saga. The one which did not fit the narrative went into the title.)

With aplomb, the writer began his fastidious and sesquipedalian missive.

Despite his zeal at the nefarious motive for his eclectic word choices, he astutely hid it behind a veneer of ineffable panache.

His Vorfreude on publication days was an intricate enigma, at times causing lethologica and a cacophony of petrichor.

St Mary's Island

By Maria Dorman

(Revisiting my grandmother's town of Whitley Bay.)

The Rotunda behind me, the sea to my right and Links on the left, I go in search of my objectives.

Sadly, I find no sign of the small formal garden I remember. On to St Mary's, then.

The sea washes over my trainers. Wish I'd checked the tide tables.

Novel Ideas

By Maria Dorman

(This mini saga was originally published in the Roses Mini Sagas Anthology 2024.)

At breakfast, trying to decide what to read later …

A Tale of two cities? Too divisive.

Having lunch and still can't decide …

Jane Eyre? A bit shortsighted.

Teatime, still uncertain …

Middlemarch? Too centre of the road.

Bedtime, not sure …

Ah, yes! My Left Foot – just right!

The Gift of a Child

By Maria Dorman

(This mini saga was originally published in the Roses Mini Sagas Anthology 2024.)

That morning the face in the locket had been vacant, the mother she had known almost gone.

That afternoon her two-year-old son Toby sat on his grandmother's lap, chattering and giggling, truly dementia unaware.

Opening the locket again, she sees her mother's twinkling eyes and mischievous smile. Tears spring unbidden.

It Could Have Been Me

By Maria Dorman

(This mini saga was originally published in the Roses Mini Sagas Anthology 2024.)

You know, it could have been me.

I was asked; was flattered and frightened in equal measure. And I really did think about it.

But I couldn't face the names they'd have called me or the bad reputation either. I just wasn't brave like Mary.

And I didn't love Joseph.

The End

By Maria Dorman

(This mini saga was originally published in the Roses Mini Sagas Anthology 2024.)

The end, when it came, stole in like a thief in the night.

Borders were closed, martial law imposed, the National Guard deployed, and aliens interred or deported. Shocked, disbelieving faces stared out of windows at a dystopian future none had ever expected.

In the Bay, the 305-foot statue wept.

New Beginnings

By Maria Dorman

(This mini saga was originally published in the Roses Mini Sagas Anthology 2024.)

Bobby had always loved soccer.

He supported his local team, just like his dad and grandad. Many a weekend was spent cheering them on, whether playing home or away.

Stepping onto the hallowed ground, Bobby's chest swells with pride.

It's his first day as an apprentice groundsman at Wembley Stadium.

Midnight at Bethlehem

By Maria Dorman

(Nobody enjoys a long sermon at the midnight Christmas Eve service. This one was written for St Peter's Old Hurst, in Cambridgeshire, whose service is held at 10pm – or midnight if you are in Bethlehem.)

The journey was long and uncomfortable, the birth even more so. We were all really frightened: me, Joseph, even the poor donkey.

But look! He's here: my son, God's son, your friend and saviour.

Look into my baby's eyes and know that God is among us and truly loves us.

Hope Springs Eternal

By Maria Dorman

Staring down the barrel of a shot gun wasn't quite how I'd imagined starting my first Saturday off in weeks. The face behind it was grim, bearded, and totally strange. Not odd, I mean he was a stranger. I didn't know him from Adam – no fig leaf, you see. Have I told you that stress makes me ramble?

It all started on Tuesday, when I realised I still had time to send a Valentine's card to Margery Phipps. This time, though, I'd decided to sign it and enclose a short note telling her how I dreamt of her day and night, and would she please be my girlfriend as I was fed up being on my own? I know that sounds weird. I didn't phrase it that way, but if you think I'd tell just anyone what I wrote to Margery, well, hm, I wouldn't want to embarrass her.

Anyway, Tuesday lunchtime I signed the note with a flourish and addressed the envelope – 32 Manningtree Close. Just made the last post from the corner by the Jug and Bluebottle. I was walking home, whistling happily, when I suddenly remembered that Margery had moved last month. I barely noticed the icy water drenching me as a bus shot past me, at least 10mph over the speed limit. What had I done? Would she ever figure me? How would she even know, idiot, I asked myself – you sent it to the wrong address.

I did try to get it back, but the house was empty. I decided to leave it and hope whoever lived in her old house now would ignore my invitation to... ahem, never mind.

Nothing happened on Wednesday, Thursday or Friday, so Saturday came as a bit of a surprise. I looked at the shotgun again, then realised I did know who was wielding it. Bloody Post Office redirections actually working properly for once!

'Hello, Mr Phipps,' I said weakly, just before I was deafened by the blast. I guess I should have known Margery was out of my league.

Goodbye

By Maria Dorman

The battered Marie Kondo sailed across the room, neatly passing the cut glass chandelier, the Dartington decanter, and an over ripe melon, to land centimetres away from a very startled cat. The feline made its displeasure known using claws, teeth and amazingly versatile vocals.

Josie O'Neill had been tidying up. Or trying to. She was finding it extremely difficult to reconcile minimalism with the need to be prepared for any eventuality. She had a reputation for always having the obscure item a friend or colleague needed, just when they needed it, and she was reluctant to lose her role.

But her life was a mess. Or rather, her home was a mess. And her office. And some (most?) of her car. She was beginning to believe she actually had things no one would recognise or want, so maybe—just maybe—it was time to slim down her belongings. She squared her shoulders and retrieved the book.

Then she started remembering things… each item she looked at brought back memories. Of holidays she had taken, jobs she had done, people she had met. The good times—and the bad—all of which had moulded her into the woman she had become. The mug that reminded her of her long-dead mother; the bag her sister had given her, the souvenir from Singapore. Useful things she didn't really need but liked to have around.

Josie drew herself up, took a deep breath and announced to the cat—who viewed her with suspicion—that she was damned if she was getting rid of everything. 'I will, however, dispense of a minimum of 10% of my belongings,' she said, trying to sound important and as if she meant it (which she really did). 'And,' she said dramatically stabbing a finder in the direction of the frazzled feline, 'I will begin with this…'

It had been a bargain, and something she really thought would change her life. 'Goodbye, good buy,' she called, as she hurled Marie Kondo expertly into the waste bin.

GRASP

By Maria Dorman

Gordon slid the patio Door open cautiously. Disturbing the neighbours would be most counterproductive. Under the baleful eye of a waning moon, he made his way to the summerhouse at the end of the garden.

*

Rosemary tripped over her dressing gown belt, blundered into an armchair and generally made enough noise to seriously disturb the dead. A pause to see if anyone had heard her... no movement... and so she tapped her way down the garden path

*.

Aloysius gently shook **S**tevie awake. 'Time to go, my dear,' he whispered, then had to repeat the words twice more with increasing volume, until his message was received. Husband and wife slipped out of the door by the kitchen.

*

Paulo straightened his tie and shrugged on his jacket; picking up his stick in one had and a torch in the other. His eyes weren't getting any younger, and neither did he trust the moonlight to provide sufficient illumination.

*

Gordon cleared his throat with exaggerated importance. 'Ladies and gentlemen,' he said with barely a hint of pomposity, 'I declare the inaugural meeting of GRASP—Gentlefolk Rebelling Against Sadistic Policies—officially in session.'

Once Past the Blue Moon

By Maria Dorman

Someone walked over my grave as I left the pub. I tried to shrug off the feeling, blaming the chill of a late spring evening, but the feeling persisted. I glanced around. Nothing. Well, nothing unexpected. Just shadowy streets with inadequate lighting and the odd passer-by on the other side of the road. I could hear the hum of traffic in the distance, the occasional 'neenaw' of an emergency vehicle creating a counterpoint. I walked on, deliberately sauntering, rebellious to the last.

It had been an odd evening, filled with anticipation and excitement, ending in anti-climax. I doubted I would see the group again. Correction. I hoped I would, but couldn't see it happening, somehow. Boats had been burnt tonight and I was the one who had tossed the match.

Is it wrong to tell the truth? On reflection, maybe honesty wasn't always the best policy. Did I make a mistake? I guess time will tell, but I couldn't bear any more of the platitudes or the hedging around things. The artificial pleasantness and 'encouragement' had begun to feel more like a subtle stab in the back. Sod diplomacy. Time for spades to be spades, not garden implements for moving quantities of soil. Tonight was the night I told the truth, clearly (with examples, of course) and gave up pussyfooting around creative egos.

It didn't go well. It didn't go well at all.

Amy didn't seem at all impressed when I suggested she should tone down the descriptive drivel in her piece. I mean, cerulean ether? Really? Blue sky, woman, blue sky. You aren't Wordsworth!

Then there was Davy's dialogue: if people spoke like his characters I-would-be-convinced-I-had-stumbled-into-the-robot-apocalypse. Even zombies sound more human than his characters. Give them some life, man!

And Tilly. Oh Tilly, your rambling sentences are tortuous. Random thoughts spill onto pages, there is a national shortage of analgesic. The hero is a wimp, her appendix burst, septicaemia killed Brian. Punctuation is added with mathematical precision as an afterthought, semi colons are non-existent. Don't you realise your disconnected verbiage will have made H_____ cranky? She hates comma splices, hates them with a, well, with hatred.

I must admit, though, that I felt a touch of guilt when I thought about the feedback I'd given Daisy. I like Daisy and I like her stories. I was genuinely trying to be helpful when I suggested that perhaps her five-foot-nothing, seven-stone senior citizen would be unlikely to overpower and stab to death a healthy forty-something woman, even if she did creep up behind her one dark night. I sighed. Maybe I should apologise to Daisy. Her stories were meant to entertain, not reflect reality, albeit she clearly saw herself as an avenging pensioner.

I had just passed the Blue Moon when I heard something behind me. As I turned there was a glint in the feeble light and a searing pain caught my breath.

'Told you so.'

MY END

The Importance of House Training

By Maria Dorman

The doorbell rings just as I sit down for my morning coffee. A quick peak through the side window shows a pair of red cheeks and a grimace that would strike fear into a gargoyle. If I had one, that is.

Sighing, I go to the door, open it halfway and peer round at my neighbour.

'Miss Kelsey,' she begins, 'I'm speechless.'

I think about correcting her, but past experience kicks me up the backside, so I simply smile weakly and try to drum up some soothing response. Mind blank—anomia strikes. 'Um,' I manage.

'Miss Kelsey, it won't do all,' she says, with all the power of a retired headmistress. 'Philbert has been in my nettle bed again.'

'Oh dear…'

'And if that wasn't bad enough, he's singed Thomas's whiskers, and the hens have stopped laying.'

'Ah, right, Philbert.' What on earth am I supposed to say in response. 'How is Thomas?' I enquire, hoping to distract her with my uncharacteristic concern for her mangy tabby.

'He's gone to ground in the coal hole!' she shouts. 'How do you think he is?'

Now *I'm* speechless.

'If you can't control that creature of yours,' she bellows, 'then I'll report you to the Society.'

And now I'm getting worried. 'Please, Mrs Jones, please don't shout. You know it upsets Philbert.' Philbert getting upset is to be avoided at all costs. To say he gets heated is an understatement.

'Poppycock, fiddlesticks, balderdash…'

Mrs Jones has a very colourful vocabulary. Sometimes I think it would be better if she simply blasphemes, but there it is. I try again to calm her. 'Mrs Jones, I really do suggest…'

Too late. A moment later a little pile of ash on my doorstep is all that remains. 'Philbert! Bad dragon! Back to your cave immediately.' Glancing around, I see the street is empty and turn to pick up the dustpan and brush.

Winging It

By Maria Dorman

Deirdre shut her eyes tight and stifled a scream. A quick peek showed her that the situation hadn't changed: she really was hovering near Mrs Higginbottom's cracked and crumbling chimney. If only she didn't hate heights so much. The breeze caught the smoke from the chimney and flicked it at her, so that she found herself coughing and sneezing like a veteran hay fever sufferer.

She thought about screaming for help, but a quick glimpse of the feathers moving gently somewhere in the region of her right scapula made her realise that perhaps anonymity was the better option. She tried to relax into the experience. Somehow, though, she found the reality of being thirty feet or more in the air and at the mercy of what she suspected were a pair of rather impressive wings, was more than she could manage.

A sob escaped her. 'I want to go home,' she moaned, then stifled a scream as she shot through the air like an arrow and dived towards…

That wasn't her house. It looked more like… 'The Zoo?' she squealed, as a tiger approached at great speed. At the last minute the wings executed an incredible turn, and she gracefully joined the elephants as they had their daily bath.

There was a moment of sheer panic as the water erupted from the nearest trunk but another impossible manoeuvre from the feathered accessories set her down gently at the coffee shop.

'I'll have a double espresso, please,' she managed in a shaky voice, 'and go easy on the water.' A white feather floated down onto the table and slowly faded away in the sunshine.

Smudge

By Maria Dorman

The unexpected arrival turned up on our doorstep one Tuesday morning, just after 10 o'clock. I remember the time because I had just finished my second cup of coffee and washed up the cafetiere. It's true, predictability is one of my (many) failings.

She was hungry and thirsty, and seemed desperate for social contact. After a little milk and a small tin of tuna, she settled on my lap, kneading my legs with her tiny pincushion claws, before sleeping so soundly that I had to check her chest movements to be sure she was still with me. So much for my normal Tuesday morning activities.

Within a week, she was an established member of the household, with a litter tray and feeding station in the utility room, and an armchair in the living room that she had requisitioned on her first day. Neither of us could imagine life without her, but we couldn't quite decide what to call her. None of the names we tried were quite right. Somehow, we defaulted to 'Cat', clearly channelling our inner *Red Dwarf*.

Oddly enough, although she was very patient with us, I could have sworn she almost glared every time we called her 'Cat'. 'If only you could talk,' I told her, 'you could tell us what your name is. It's obvious you don't really want to be 'Cat' forever.' She looked like she agreed then wandered off to the garden (utilising the newly installed 'Cat' flap to beat the bounds of her territory).

Eventually we all forgot about trying to find out her real name. We'd also never managed to find out where she had come from that Tuesday morning. For a while I'd worried that some irate fellow pensioner might turn up on our doorstep and demand the return of their feline. But no, she was ours. Or rather, we were hers.

One morning I decided to try out 'Marmite' as a moniker. I thought it might work, as it sort of went with some of her colouring. The look she gave me made me realise that in the love it/hate it stakes, she was a definite hater!

And then, last Saturday afternoon, Bob was writing some cheques to pay bills. He always writes with a flashy gold fountain pen and as he signed the last cheque 'Cat' leapt into action, attacking the flashing prey, and spattering ink everywhere.

Wiping black ink from his face, Bob began to laugh. 'That' it,' he said triumphantly. 'Cat's name is Smudge.'

And it was!

Bullet

By Maria Dorman

The scenery passes in a blur of speed. Kim—artist and author—is far away in another land, dreaming of fabulous creatures with blue, green, purple iridescent skin and fiery temperaments.

One such behemoth is an outcast – eschewed by his compatriots because he despises gold.

'Unnatural,' they cry. 'Traitor,' shout others. Even his siblings hiss at him as he passes. A few drops of accelerant fall like tears.

Sunlight slides over unbearably beautiful wings as he glides over green slopes towards snow-capped mountains beckoning in the distance. Spying the silver snake, he pounces.

Daily Telegraph, Tuesday

Mythical Beast Bites Bullet

Shona Gilchrist

She enjoys writing stories, making up stories, reading stories, watching stories, listening to stories and excels at procrastination. Until this anthology, none of her work had been published. Unless, a dissertation counts, work blogs and documentation count or updating out-of-copywrite plays count?

Shona enjoys letting her creative juices flow through amateur dramatic musicals and farces - back-stage and on stage, directing and being the most important part in any performance; a bum-on-seat.

She is enthusiastically 'helped' with her numerous crafting hobbies, particularly the needle work, by her housemate Scrabble, the tallon-tastic Maine Coon cat.

To My Own Surprise

By Shona Gilchrist

(I'd never written a poem. To my surprise, I went along to a talk by Bea at Swanwick about poetry. She discussed Kennings. To my surprise, I joined in with the exercise to write some Kennings. As others read out their Kennings, I realised, to my surprise, that what I had written could constitute a poem. And now I include the result here, very much to my own surprise!)

Hello Scrabble

You're my ...
        laser-chaser
        trill-trumpeter
        catnap-virtuoso
        daily-playmate

Despite your ...
        midnight-zooming
        spider-crunching
        curtain-climbing
        chaos-mongering

Even with your ...
        death-staring
        skin-ripping
        laser-focussed
        talon-wielding

You're still my
        floofy-britches
        purr-monster
        cuddle-bunny
        daily-joy

Last Time I saw Him He …

By Shona Gilchrist

(10 minute timed write, with the title as the prompt.)

OMG! I just stood and stared. That was John Tilbury. He had been the school crush when we were at sixth form. I had sat next to him in chemistry just before the end of year dance. He'd just broken up with his girlfriend and therefore didn't have a date for the dance, so he'd asked me.

John Tilbury had asked me, me, to the dance! I remember I was so excited, I'd got a new dress, spent 3 hours at the hairdressers and nearly fainted with excitement when he'd rung the doorbell to pick me up.

That had been a magical night. We danced, we laughed, we drank, and we laughed and danced some more.

Then the whole gang had gone our separate ways and most of us lost touch when we'd gone to university.

And now, here in this coffee shop serving me coffee was John Tilbury. Large as life, John Tilbury.

'Jo Flannigan, is that you?' he said as his face broke into a huge grin. Oh, be still my beating heart, I thought. Here was my biggest crush in front of me again.

'Are you on your own?' he asked. 'If so, I'm on a break in 5 minutes, we could catch up.'

My heart beat faster, I nodded and found an empty table.

He came over a few minutes later. We had a very polite chat, a few questions, a few answers and a lot of 'lovely's'.

Turns out you can't turn the clock back. He's still gorgeous, but that night was a magical end to sixth form and it will stay as just that. It can't be repeated.

Life has chapters and John Tilbury, as lovely as he was, wouldn't be in my next chapter.

Love Letter

By Shona Gilchrist

(A 10 minute timed write with the prompt of; a confession of love letter gets delivered to the wrong address ...)

Mike took a deep breath and slid the envelope under the door. He then let out a huge side relief and made his way back along the corridor to his own room. To his horror, the hall light was switched on

'Hey Mike' whispered Kate 'what are you doing in the dark?'

'Just getting a glass of water' mumbled Mike.

'Oh' said Kate 'I thought I saw you outside of Julian's room.'

'Julian's room?' No no, no ... his mind screamed. 'Umm no I was umm ... I was outside of Joan's room ...'

'Oh OK, it looked like Julian's room to me. Anyway I need a glass of water myself.' Mike then found himself following Kate to the kitchen to grab a glass of water.

Mike then spent the majority of the night pacing. He was far too worried to go to sleep. If he'd pushed his love letter under Julian's door, he'd never hear the end of it. He eventually lay down, dreading the morning and cursing his cowardice of not telling Joan to her face.

The next morning he kept his door ajar, waiting for Julian's light to go on. He still wasn't sure what he was going to do but he was desperate to get to Julian before he read that letter.

'Morning' said Kate, as she passed his room. He dived back behind his door. Then he heard Kate knock at a door and yell at Julian to let her in.

Mike paced around his room painting a new mental picture of Julian and Kate reading his letter and laughing at him.

Next thing Kate was back at his door. 'Idiot, tell her to her face.' She then thrust his letter into his hands.

'You owe me one.' She chuckled as she went back to her own room.

I'm Ready

By Shona Gilchrist

(A 10 minute timed write with the prompt; your heart has been closed for too long. You open up, but where did it get you?)

I stared at the warm deposit. I could actually see the steam coming off it in the cold January air. Oh well, I thought this is what I signed up for. I bent over and grabbed the alarmingly warm, brown, steaming pile. I wrapped it up into the obligatory bag and tied a knot. The cute little face just looked at me and blinked.

'It's what I'm supposed to do.' I unnecessarily explained as I looked around for an appropriate bin. I spied one over in the corner of the field and started to wander over.

A bark made me spin round. I couldn't see Misty. I called her name. I frantically called her name. I started running and stopped when I realised I didn't know where to run to.

Then more barking. I saw Misty. I growled at her whilst she growled at the tree. I looked up and saw a squirrel looking down at us.

Annoyingly there was no fear at all in the cheeky face. I felt the little chap knew very well that he was safe from both of us whilst in that tree.

'Come on,' I said, picking up the lead as we made our way back to the office. Tracy saw us coming back and waved hello.

'How did it go?' she asked.

'Yeah, you were right, I am ready to have another dog,' I said with a contented sigh.

Mind Made Up

By Shona Gilchrist

(10 minute timed write with the prompt; you have to do this.)

She stared at it. Not again. She guessed this was the time of year for them. She didn't move. But if she didn't do anything, it might just vanish and that would be worse.

Slowly she put out her right hand and extended it to the coffee table. Not for one second taking an eye off the creature. Her hand found the glass. She picked it up and brought it into her peripheral vision. There was some slightly pale yellow liquid in there. She didn't remember that being there. What was that liquid?

Dratted cat, why on earth would it pee in a glass! Her mind spun. Where could she dump this liquid. She froze. The spider had gone.

She was standing on the sofa by the time she spied it again. It was now in the perfect position. But there wasn't another container that she could use to catch the spider. Without here really realising what she was doing she brought the glass to her face and sniffed the liquid. Oh the relief broke free from her as a low drawn out release of air. It was just the herbal tea from last night.

She drank down the cold liquid and drew in a long breath. This was it. She braced herself. Come on, it's a tiny thing. It's more scared of you, than you are of it. Just as she stepped forward and raised the glass, the cat pounced and crunched.

'You horrid but wonderful kitty' she said as the cat looked back at her with a 'wot' expression in his eyes and eight legs flailing from his mouth.

Bats

By Shona Gilchrist

(A 15 minute timed write with the prompt; Bats wake you up from your slumber.)

'Ok, here's your oil skins' he said, 'pop your sleeping bags inside and that's you ready to go.'

'But where's the tent' squealed Jessica.

'You don't need a tent in the Outback' said Paul. We're hardy here in the Outback, like cowboys, we sleep under the stars. Now get your beds ready and we'll start the evening meal on the fire.'

Once the beds were laid, if shoving a sleeping bag into a oil skin and arranging them in the line, was bed-laying, they gathered around the campfire.

'Now we're going to make bread and soup' Paul informed them all. He set Jessica and Felicity making the bread whilst Tanya & Rose chopped the vegetables for the soup.

The soup was being made in a pot hung from a tripod over the fire. To Jessica's horror the bread was being made by literally burying it in the embers on one side of the fire. She'd calmed down when she was assured that the inside will taste wonderful and it was only the outside that would touch the fire embers.

Sure enough, by the time the soup was ready and the bread was baked, even Jessica had to admit, it was a lovely meal.

Well fed, they clambered into their oil skin wrapped sleeping bags and slowly fell asleep.

'ARGH' they all woke up in shock at the noise.

‘What was it’? ‘What happened?’ ‘Who screamed?’ They all clamoured at once. Jessica was hysterical.

‘Something hit my face. It touched me. What was it? Get it off me.’

Paul shone his torch at her face and smiled, explaining that there was nothing there. He showed her a reflection of herself when she didn't believe him

‘It was just a bat’ he said soothingly. ‘They were just flying out for the night. They’re all gone now.’

Everyone climbed back into their sleeping bags, except Jessica.

‘Would you prefer to sleep on the couch for the rest of the night Jessica?’

‘Yes please Uncle Paul. Your back garden adventures are always too wild for me.’

The Inspector Calls

By Shona Gilchrist

(Inspired by a 10 minute timed write with the theme; You pull up to the Farm. The first thing you notice is a duck approaching your car.)

'Quack, quack'

OMG, she thought. I nearly ran over a duck. She was nervous. This was her first inspection on her own. So killing a duck, however accidental, would not look good on the paperwork.

She got out the car, collected her notebook, straightened her new Barber jacket and walked over to the cottage. She squelched through the mud and tried very hard not to think of all that mud on her new boots.

She knocked on the door which fell open as she did so. She poked her head around the door and yelled 'Mr Hopkins. Hello Mr Hopkins. It's the environmental inspector, may I come in?'

She stood in the doorway, very unsure of what to do next. She looked around. Then she saw the feet.

'Oh my goodness, Mr Hopkins.' She ran over to the settee and saw a man, face down on the floor.

'Mr Hopkins, are you OK?' she yelled as she lent down next to him and shook his shoulders as she'd been taught to do in her recent first aid course.

There was no response from him, but at least he is breathing, she thought as she looked and felt around for signs of blood. With none found, she took a deep breath to calm herself. She then pulled out her mobile and rang for an ambulance. She realised how shaken she was when she heard her own voice falter and saw the notebook wavering as she read out the address.

She paced around the room and kept staring out the window, waiting for the ambulance to arrive. But she still jumped when the sirens turned into the farmyard.

The arrival of the paramedics, to their departure with Mr Hopkins, went by in a blur. As soon as the paramedics had asked her a few questions, they focussed on their patient. All she could do was watch, horrified at the scene in front of her. She hadn't even offered them a cup of tea. Not that she knew where the kitchen was, but wasn't that what 'one' did in these situations?

When they had gone, she just stood by her car wondering what to do. Was there a Mrs Hopkins? Should she leave a note. What would she write? The duck didn't seem qualified to pass on a message.

Thankfully she heard a tractor turn into the farmyard. The farmer jumped down and apologised.

'You must be the inspector. Sorry I'm late. I'm Mr Hopkins.'

Bea Hutchings

From an original painting by Bea

Bea lives by the sea and the River Dart in Devon, with her husband and crazy dog Chewy.

She writes poetry, short stories, articles, and although currently writing a crime novel, she also enjoys writing comedy and romance, blending humour and satire with a dash of psychology.

Bea enjoys acting, stand-up comedy, spoken word and is an experienced artist.

Her writing has been published online and in magazines, including Writing Magazine, Acumen, Orbis. Heads, Hearts & Tails, Stories and Poetry.

Mother's Elastic Stockings

By Bea Hutchings

(This poem has travelled around the world on cruise ships. It has been used onboard the ship in writing tutorials as an example of writing a memoir poem. It has also been published in Heads, Hearts & Tails, A Distillery of Poetry and Stories.)

Mother perches on quilted eiderdown,
with an Elastoplast stocking rolled
inside out, pulled up her arm, wishing
her legs were as smooth, as easy

to negotiate over the damp, hot,
tenderness. She remembers silk stockings,
her American pilot killed in action,
as if silk thread can pull a memory

from her outstretched arm, entwine
locked hands, draw up the corners
of her smile into lasting kisses like
gum he chewed, spearmint on candy.

With effort, she hooks a stocking
over crooked toes, calcified nails,
a swollen foot. Gingerly rolling
over thromboses and varicose veins,

to the rhythm of tuba, saxophone,
the Glenn Miller Orchestra
until she reaches top note. Almost tight,
almost secure. One, Flying Fortress

held high by a garter, with a twist
and a sixpence, or the dime she kept
to button her heart.

Prolific Procrastination

By Bea Hutchings

(First published in a Swanwick Newsletter.)

Find me the perfect pen, the type which never leaks or smudges,

that I might dribble dastardly doodles across the pristine

virgin pages of my Swanwick notebook, scribbling notary nonsense with the voracious appetite of a plucked scarab beetle.

Let me bustle through the bookroom amidst murders and mystery, capturing the fragrant torture of desperate deadlines, dangling

like persistent hemorrhoids, hovering thirstily

with herculean relish,

above the rampant chapters of a ferocious edit.

Show me the tell of an author furrowing with their fringed foibles and petulant punctuation, wearily wandering through memoir and sleepless nights, slithering through drafts and puddles of perpetually induced perspiration.

And I want to hug them. Throw my arms around them

and participate with consonants of encouragement,

rattling my words over my tongue like a bag of randomly selected scrabble tiles.

I want to laugh and sing until my face aches, and my body wobbles like a buskering tsunami that lasts five hundred words, or more.

I want to see old friends and embrace the panic of writerly block with fructiferous literary appetite.

Let me create characters in rooms filled with Swanickers and Knickerswans.

Where hairdos and dancing, dilly-dallies among workshops and websites, networks, and badgered newbies.

And I want to sing, like a sixty's soprano, or a poppin' good chimney sweep:

'Pen penalty, pen penalty, pen, pen don't chew, when booking times are open

I'll be joining the queue - Pen penalty, pen penalty, pen, pen, pen don't chew,

I need a new pen and only Swanwick's will do.'

Up tempo, and with gusto, friends -

next August I'll be there…

Hold it, hold it…vibrato, vibrato… (optional)…

and see you there too!'

PS Please excuse the singing – I think I just swallowed a promulgation. Bea x

Oh, I do like to be beside the Seaside

By Bea Hutchings

(Winner Poetry Swanwick / Writing Magazine 2023)

Wrap me inside a golden sweet paper, the one that drools

with the taste of summer, or the bite of a juicy ripe plum

as it dribbles down my chin like brecciated marble

through the valleys and wrinkles of an overcooked suntan.

Let me crunch on a sherbet lemon or blackcurrant bonbon,

and let me lick the sticky granules and sugar crystals

from lips kissed with passion fruit or smooched in coconut balm.

Twist me along the promenade in a babble of rag-time music,

midst the menacing hawking from petulant, chip-stealing seagulls,

and fishy-warm air, rich with the tang of cockles and vinegar.

Sit me on the top of a castle with sea bubbles tickling

between my toes, and salty-red sand sticking to shimmering pearls,

or diamonds, dripping through the layers of my sea-flushed ripples.

Hold me in your outstretched hands until I melt,

escaping through ice-cream fingers, or swimming

in a rock-pool of candy scented memories, drenched

in the skinny-dip of a silky, drunken midnight.

Spin me in the whispering floss of succulent strawberries,

dipped in Jamaican-rum chocolate, or blood-orange liqueur,

and I want to drown in the fragrant, lingering holiday of olive oil

and sun-blushed tomatoes, vine leaves and blackberry wine,

relishing that Mackintosh moment when you tell me you love me.

I want to roll around your mouth like a vintage bingo ball,

skittling over your garlic infused tongue, rampaging

through the mercurial, cavernous holes, peppered in the silver

of your amalgam fillings until,

you startled me awake, damp with sweat from my frivolous stupor,

rubbing crisp crustaceans from my eyes as you reach the crescendo of your gargantuan snores, or the rumbling, tumbling vibrations rising and falling in a Richter Scale snort, or a squealing high-pitched fluffer-doodle, like the ones erupting

from the pinched end of a half-deflated balloon.

You are mummified. Tangled in a swathe of seaweed and samphire,

wrapped in the arcadian cloak of a postcard town.

And I turn my head and look at you and all I can say is -

'Did you put the bins out?'

Sweet Dreams are Made of This

By Bea Hutchings

(Winner 500 Word Flash Fiction story South Hams Authors Network Literary Festival 2023)

Winter bites my neck as rain slithers into ice, and I taste the gag of cold, wet pavements and dank raincoats as people scurry by. I'm alone, waiting for the bus, too cold to run. A trickle slips beneath my up-turned collar and briefly, I think about him:

The silk of his fingertips as he kisses tiny white hairs along my spine, teasing lips brushed over my thin, piccolo bones; heat from his breath, warms me, as his hands softly cup my breasts; a practised tongue excites my childhood scars, tracing them back to where we first met in the school playground, where we whistled gap-toothed promises.

Tender times, when our innocence led us to believe we were invincible or could wrap the worries of the world in a King-sized feather duvet; live forever, cosily togged together.

Our bed, still hot and rumpled, as the man I never knew punctured my life; squeezed his long fingers around my neck, choked me. His right fist held inches from my face, waiting for the poison words he spat at me to demolish everything I believed he was or had ever been.

'I'm leaving you. You understand?! I'm in love with Kiara.'

His lover. My sister. Who had cuddled under our duvet while a surgeon unhooked my womb, my life.

Wailing sirens pull me back from my reverie. My travel case sits clumsily between my thighs, shielded from a thunderous deluge with my long, black, coat. Hailstones dance on pathways. Empty crisp packets swirl towards overflowing drains; and I barely recognise the shop behind me I once owned. Cracks zigzag across smeared windows; piss ferments in the doorway. I peer inside. A poster curls under the weight of decaying insects. Lopsided pictures of herbs and spices take me back to my mother's cooking. Home:

I shut my eyes, imagine myself at the bazaar; the seller's banter, fun, paper bags rustling. I pick coriander and blue fenugreek sprung fresh from the mountains, inhale the heady scent of pepper. My family sing folksongs, share ghost stories, wag fingers; warnings I chose to ignore of nightshade and bitterness. About him.

My distorted reflection stares back at me. My hands tremble as I touch the bare patch above my ear. His parting gift as he pulled my head back to kiss my lips, my neck, my shoulders, one more time. His shocked face as I slit his throat with the silver handled knife my mother gave me long ago. His lovers name forever on his tongue.

A weak sun breaks through the purple-bruised clouds, as the storm blows over. A ray of light shines on the window as my bus arrives. An advertisement reflected in the shop window says, 'Luxurious-Feather-Duvet. Sweet Dreams are made of this.'

I smile as I open my travel bag to find a newspaper parcel. A bloodied knife lies buried inside it. I post it through the shops rusty letter box and head towards the bus. Wolves prowl. It's raining. Siren's wail.

The Library of Forgotten Grammar

By Bea Hutchings

Lend me a sonnet, the one without rhyme
and let me scuttle amongst the vowels and syllables
in a puncture of commas and colons,
on a random selection of discord and frustration,

and let me scuttle amongst the vowels and syllables
on a random selection of discord and frustration
riding on the back of a humped back hyphen
as it rolls off the tongue like a nuanced noun

on a random selection of discord and frustration
as it rolls off the tongue like a nuanced noun
write me a pantoum with its repeated lines
and strange behaviour as it ladders constructive stanzas

as it rolls off the tongue like a nuanced noun
and strange behaviour as it ladders constructive stanzas
hooking a comma on the rung, the rising of a dot,
dashing the hyphen with belligerent boldness

and strange behaviour as it ladders constructive stanzas
dashing the hyphen with belligerent boldness
like a meteoric sword, slashing the skin of consonance
and iambic pentameter in a dazzling underscore

dashing the hyphen with belligerent boldness
and iambic pentameter in a dazzling underscore
as I borrow a hash, so I might explore the complexities
of tags and tweets, or the conjuncture of flow and metre
and iambic pentameter in a dazzling underscore
of tags and tweets, or the conjuncture of flow and metre
from a precipitous member of vowel and consonant,
a firm of literary solicitors with stiff upper case and capital requirement,

of tags and tweets, or the conjuncture of flow and metre
from a firm of literary solicitors with stiff upper case and capital requirement
taking me to the punctuated section where grammar grows like metamorphic interconnections, overloaded with bumptious metaphor

from a firm of literary solicitors with stiff upper case and capital requirement.
taking me to the punctuated section where grammar grows like
simultaneous similes vying for attention,
waving with free-handed ellipsis and double-twisted apologies

taking me to the punctuated section, where grammar grows,
where simultaneous similes are vying for attention,
in a lexicon of frustration and misspelled allegory
wiggling the fish along a well-spaced line in a bold calligraphy

taking me to the punctuated section, where grammar grows like
a lexicon of frustration and misspelled allegory
of squid ink and coarse registers, or a flick of an italic tail
in a conundrum of suggestive, repetitive incantations.

where simultaneous similes are vying for attention
wiggling the fish along a well-spaced line in a bold calligraphy.
in a puncture of commas and colons.
Lend me a sonnet, the one without rhyme.

Furniture Disorder

By Bea Hutchings

Sometimes I think I'm a drawer,
Open, close, open, close,
Stuff things in,
Yank things out
Dust off and hoover,
Sometimes empty,
Full of old rubbish
Overloaded.
But I do have very nice handles.

Drop Stitched!

By Bea Hutchings

(Created after a friend said how tight her knitting was on the needle! There are follow-up stories, which also contain her creative pursuits.)

'Knitting, that's what I'll do,' Julie thought, 'use up all those odd bits of wool I bought in the charity shop.'

She rummaged in her sewing box for a pair of size twelve needles, pricking her finger on the sharp end of a loose needle in the bottom of the box, and fell asleep.

When she woke up, a knitted panda bear was sitting in the armchair opposite her.

'You can't knit' he said, in a rather strange, strangled voice. 'Look at the state of me. You squeezed all the stitches on the knitting needle so tight, I've ended up with a corkscrew neck and a lopsided face!'

Julie stared at him. 'I only dropped a few stitches' she said, 'and you don't look *that* bad.'

'You said that about my father, and he was almost castrated!'

'Sorry,' she said, 'maybe I should stay off the gin in the afternoons.'

The panda stared at her.

'You're not really talking to me at all are you?' Julie said.

'No. I can't feckin' breathe for one thing, I haven't got a mouth, just a row of wobbly garter stitches, and I can't pee either, because someone stuffed me full of laddered tights!'

‘Maybe knitting’s not my thing after all?’

‘No.’

I Didn't Know I'd Lost You 'til I Found You!

By Bea Hutchings

(This poem is based on a true story and contains elements that some people might find, or have found disturbing.)

My bra was missing. Lost somewhere,

in a world of DDs with impossible hooks and clasps,

negotiated by navel-skimming, bra-swivelling perspiration.

But I didn't know I'd lost you 'til I found you.

Dear bra, who had missed the morning caresses of plumpage

and plumage, jiggling and wriggling, kneading and squeezing,

swearing, and rolling like a bowling-ball

in the fast-lane of clattering milk-bottle expressionism,

or friction-in-motion joggers nipple.

O bra! O pink and brown spotted freckle-plopper,

laced with embroidery anglaise,

I didn't know I'd lost you 'til I found you.

You were trapped inside the bosom of an old bed, hooked

to the framework of a King-sized, not so silent night,
chained to the white fibres, waiting for your Knight in shining ardour

to release you.

Forlorn and forgotten, you lay there until,

the day the bedsprings died,

and the dungeon of drawers were whipped out,

and yes, I found you! surrounded by long lost knickers,

Pippa pee-throughs without a wisp of gusset,

which I once tried to dry under the grill, and no, they didn't catch fire,

they singed and snapped,

but I saved them just in case of emergencies.

O bra! You were safe, cocooned in the girth of a pair of lucky,

rainbow-striped, budgie smuggling underpants.

O bra! O how I've missed you.

But I didn't know I'd lost you 'til I found you.

You can sod off now. Swing out the door.

You're the one who left me with saggy boobs dragging on the floor,

and I stumbled, I stood on them in surprise.

You left me with tears pooling in my eyes,

and long ago, like I must have said before,

O bra! O lacy bra, disaster.

You don’t fit me anymore.

Martin Lake

Martin Lake lives in Dorset with his wife, one of their daughters, and their dog, Bonnie. Balancing a busy family life and a career as Head of IT, he carves out time to pursue his passion for storytelling.

Inspired by Arthurian legends, Norse mythology, and a love of classic fantasy fiction, he wrote his debut novel *Beyond the Stones*, which was published in 2024.

In addition to writing, Martin has delivered workshops at various writing festivals. *Sunny Side Up* marks his second appearance in a short story anthology, following his contribution to *This Little World*.

Just in Time for Christmas

By Martin Lake

The wind attacked mercilessly, whipping his robes around him. Fine particles of sand scoured his skin, penetrating everywhere, even places he thought shouldn't be penetrated. Scratching at his discomfort, he plodded on sullenly.

'Are you still angry with me?' asked a small voice from somewhere slightly above his right shoulder. The tone was a mixture of apprehension and exasperation. Joseph glanced up at Mary for a moment, seated on the small donkey.

'Why would I be angry with you?' he answered bitterly. 'Oh, unless you mean the fact that my wife is carrying a baby that isn't mine. That when we were betrothed, she got herself knocked up. Could that possibly be it?'

'I've told you time and time again. It wasn't like that. I never went with any man. It was an immaculate conception.'

Joseph snorted. 'Well, I've heard the lads down the synagogue club rate it out of 10 before, but I've never heard anyone call it immaculate.'

Mary sighed, shifting carefully to ease her discomfort. 'I've told you what happened. The Holy Spirit descended upon me and begat me with child.'

'*Begat me with child*, what sort of talk is that?'

'It means that I have been chosen to be the mother of the Son of God, the Messiah.'

Joseph glared up at her, 'He's not the Messiah, and you're a very naughty girl!'

'Look,' said Mary, all trace of timidity now replaced by annoyance, 'you didn't have to go through with the wedding. You could have broken off our betrothal.'

'Yeah, right,' sarcasm lacing his tone, 'as if that was really an option after your dad sent that big fella round to have a word with me.'

'That was the Angel Gabriel.'

'I don't care who it was. Having some enormous bloke turning up in your bedroom in the middle of the night is enough to put the frighteners up anyone. And then when he practically threatened me…'

'He didn't threaten you!'

'Well, it felt like it. I wasn't about to take any chances.'

'When will you get it through your thick carpenter's skull? The child I am carrying is the Son of God. He will reign over the House of Israel and bring peace to the world.'

'Well, I wish he'd start by bringing me a second donkey. My feet are killing me,' Joseph quipped petulantly.

Mary threw him a look.

'So how is young Timmy supposed to change the world then?' asked Joseph.

'It isn't Timmy. He shall be named Jesus,' said Mary determinedly.

'Jesus?' answered Joseph incredulously. 'You're gonna call him Jesus? Christ, the poor sod will get crucified with a name like that.'

Mary's eyes suddenly had a faraway, thoughtful look. 'Jesus Christ,' she said to herself in an almost inaudible whisper.

‘What did you say?’

‘Oh, nothing,’ she replied, ‘just thinking aloud.’

‘Well,’ said Joseph, determined to have the last word, ‘you had better hope he doesn’t have a big Roman nose or something. Because if he does, then you’re on your own.’

They lapsed into an uncomfortable silence and spent the next few hours trudging silently through the wilderness.

‘Joseph. Joseph look. We’re here. Bethlehem,’ exclaimed Mary suddenly.

Joseph shielded his eyes from the glare of the late afternoon sun and squinted into the distance. A small town arose from the surrounding desert like a mirage, and his pace quickened as their journey’s end approached.

‘You did remember to book, didn’t you?’ Mary asked anxiously. ‘You know how busy it will be this time of year, and what with the census as well.’

‘Yes, of course I did.’ His anger had dissipated entirely with the weariness of the harsh travelling conditions. ‘I went into ‘*Olive Branch Travel’* and arranged everything. They even sent a dove to confirm the booking.’

They entered the small town shortly after and, after asking directions from a street beggar for the price of two mites, found their inn. The Cross & Crown didn’t look much, but by all accounts, it was comfortable and cheap. Joseph entered and resisted the temptation to have a sneaky pint before arranging their accommodation.

‘Good afternoon. Reservation for Joseph and Mary, please,’ he announced to the man behind the counter.

'Afternoon,' answered the man, looking up from the papyrus scroll he had been studying. 'Just the two of you, is it?'

'Yes, just myself and my wife,' Joseph answered, nodding towards Mary through the open door.

'I see, and is that your donkey?'

'Yes.'

The innkeeper's eyes looked troubled as he pointed towards a sign on the wall that read, *'No pets allowed.'*

Joseph looked from the sign to the donkey and then back to the man. 'It's a donkey, not a pet,' he announced incredulously.

'It's got four legs and doesn't talk. It's a pet.'

'You're kidding, right?' Joseph asked. The innkeeper shook his head.

'Look, it ain't like it's a flipping tortoise or anything.'

'Ah, well there, you see, if it were a tortoise, that wouldn't be a problem. We've got a nice little box out back just for tortoises.'

'Haven't you got a box out back that I can put the donkey in?'

'That would be a stable, sir.'

'Yes, I guess it would. Have you got one?'

'No.'

'But every inn has a stable!'

'Not this one.'

'Why not?'

‘Have you any idea of the price of property around these parts? The boss sold the stables a few years ago to a property developer. Made an absolute fortune.’

‘Look, isn’t there anything you can do, please? My wife is pregnant and due to give birth any day now.’

‘Congratulations, sir. Well done!’

‘It wasn’t me.’

‘Pardon?’ asked the innkeeper.

‘Oh, nothing. Look, can you help?’ asked Joseph pleadingly.

‘Sorry sir, but them’s the rules. I don’t make ‘em. I just have to follow them.’

‘Well, could I speak to the manager then?’

‘You want to speak to a manger?’ the innkeeper asked.

‘No, the manager.’

‘Ah, right, that makes more sense. Couldn’t understand why you would want to speak to a manger. Not that we have one, mind. What with not having a stable and all.’

Joseph took a deep breath, trying to calm his rising ire. ‘Look, can I speak to the *manager?* Please?’

‘No.’

‘Why not?’

‘He ain’t here, gone away for a few days. He knew how busy it would be, so he just upped and took off for a short break, the lucky bugger.’

Joseph turned and left the inn.

‘All sorted?’ asked Mary, but quickly realised something was amiss.

‘What’s wrong?’ she asked.

‘It’s the flipping donkey,’ he answered.

‘What about the donkey?’

‘There’s no stable.’

‘What do you mean no stable? It’s an inn. Every inn has a stable.’

‘That’s what I said, but apparently, this one doesn’t.’

‘Typical. You’ve found the only inn in the world without a stable.’ Joseph looked glum. ‘Didn’t you think to ask beforehand?’ she said. Joseph didn’t answer.

‘So, what are we going to do? The town is full to bursting, what with everyone being here for the census. And it’s Christmas as well.’

‘I know it’s bloody Christmas. You can’t walk down the street without tripping over sheep, shepherds or wise men. Look, I’m sure we can find a room somewhere.’ And with that, he grabbed the donkey’s lead and headed off down the street, kicking a sheep aside in passing.

Bethlehem wasn’t a huge town, but it did have a few inns, and they steadily worked their way through them all. At each one, they were greeted with the same response, *‘Sorry, there’s no room at the inn.’* Several of them helpfully suggested that maybe in the future, they should book ahead, which did nothing to improve Joseph’s mood.

It is getting late in the evening when, after yet another ‘No Vacancies’ sign, Joseph slumped, exhausted, against a wall. Mary still sat on the donkey, her face eloquently betraying the discomfort she felt after several gruelling days of travel, not to mention the imminent arrival of her son.

'Frankincense, get yer Frankincense here. Only 5 shekels a bottle.' The calls of the street trader permeated Joseph's tired brain. He opened his eyes and saw three men walking down the street towards them, each hawking their wares.

'Myrrh. Finest quality Myrrh. All the way from Commiphora Myrrha. Get yer genuine Myrrh here,' announced one of the men in a deep, melodious voice.

'Frankincense, just 5 shekels a bottle. Get your Christmas bargain here,' the first trader bellowed, attempting to drown out his competitor.

'Myrrh for the special lady in your life, just 4 shekels and a groat.'

The Frankincense seller glared at the Myrrh vendor, a hard stare perfected over years of disappointing sales. 'Frankincense, once-in-a-lifetime offer. Just 3 shekels a bottle.'

The Myrrh trader glared back but was quickly out-clamoured by the third street trader. 'Gold, sell your unwanted gold here. Do you need a little extra cash for Christmas? Best prices paid in the whole of Judah.'

The three traders quickly converged on Mary and Joseph, the only likely targets in the street. But before any of them could re-launch their sales patter, Joseph held up a hand. 'Excuse me,' he said, 'but do any of you gents know where we can get a room for the night, please?'

The Myrrh seller tutted to himself, 'Forgot to book ahead, did we, sir?' he asked condescendingly.

'Happens every year,' chipped in the Frankincense seller, with a knowing shake of the head.

'And with your good lady wife in the condition she is,' added the gold trader.

'Actually, I….' but Joseph trailed off. Some things just didn't warrant the effort to explain. 'Look, can you help us, please?' the pleading in his voice was mirrored in his eyes.

'Hmmm, I dunno,' said the Myrrh vendor.

'It is Christmas, you know?' said the Frankincense seller.

'And don't forget the census,' the gold trader chipped in.

'What about '*The Star Inn*'?' the Myrrh vendor said to his fellow traders. There followed several seconds of teeth sucking and head shaking.

'Look, we'll take anything,' interrupted Joseph desperately.

'Well, if you insist,' said the Myrrh vendor, 'but don't say we didn't warn you!' And the three men proceeded to give a collective set of directions to the Star Inn.

Five minutes later, Joseph and Mary were walking into the inn beneath a hand-painted sign depicting a large star.

'Good evening,' announced a jovial man behind a desk, 'how may I help you, folks?'

'We were told you might have a room available,' answered Joseph, 'just for a night or two.'

The innkeeper's smile disappeared. 'I'm really sorry. I just let my last room not 10 minutes ago to a nice Samaritan chap.'

'Ok, thanks anyway. Come on, Mary. Let's get the donkey,' said Joseph, his arm supporting his wife. Mary nodded but then gasped aloud in pain, clutching her swollen belly.

'Oh my,' exclaimed the innkeeper, noticing Mary's plight, 'you can't be wandering around the town in your condition.'

'It's ok,' said Joseph, 'we'll sort something out.'

The innkeeper looked at the couple for a moment and then said, somewhat tentatively, 'Look, I know it's not much, and I don't mean to insult you or your lovely wife, but there's a stable round the back you could stay in. Just for the night.'

Joseph looked at him. 'The stable?' he asked incredulously.

'Look, I know it's unusual, but you really aren't going to find anything else available tonight. And it's not like it's damp or draughty. It's practically brand new. My missus, you see, is into this sustainable smallholding lark. She's got a cow, a few sheep and a couple of goats. Oh, and a lovely little organic veg patch out back. So I built her a state-of-the-art stable. Cost me a bloody fortune, but it makes her happy.'

'Please, Joseph,' said Mary, 'let's just look at it, can we?' Her voice was small and stained, and Joseph looked down at his wife with genuine concern.

He nodded, and the innkeeper led them through a back door into the yard at the rear of the inn. As the innkeeper strode over and threw open the doors, the stable did indeed look like a magnificent edifice. The couple approached and halted on the threshold, looking into the brightly lit stable.

'Look, Mary,' Joseph said with new enthusiasm, 'it even has a manager.'

'A manager?' she queried.

'Sorry, I meant a manger.' And with that, the couple entered the stable just as the bells chimed midnight.

It was Christmas Day.

The Cloud

By Martin Lake

The man sat on the grassy hillside overlooking the lake, gazing aimlessly at the single cloud meandering across the clear azure sky. A flash of inspiration struck him. Smiling, he dipped a quill into the inkwell and wrote;

I wandered lonely as a cloud.

It was good, very good even. It was the sort of line that might take on the persona of fame all by itself, surviving through history and often being quoted.

But it wasn't entirely true. The Cloud didn't wander, and it definitely was not lonely.

At this very moment, it was off to meet with some friends for their favourite pastime: raining on Grimsby. Why Grimsby? Nobody knew. It was just the place they habitually chose for a bit of light-hearted precipitation.

Lonely indeed! Why it had lots of friends.

Admittedly, in its youth, it had been bullied, never quite fitting in with the others. It was not white and fluffy enough to be part of the chic crowd, but it was not dark and grey enough to be part of the storm-cloud elite. The cloud had been more of a dishwater grey and indistinctly shaped.

But then it discovered a hidden talent. Whilst its' rain was pitiful and its thunder mediocre, it could produce the most impressive lightning imaginable. *Unheard of for its size,* the cloud had once overheard.

And so the Cloud now had many friends and was indignant that the strange little human would think it lonely. Grimsby, now a forgotten memory, the little cloud vented its wrath on the human with some personal precipitation.

Animal Magic

By Martin Lake

Vanessa De Saragon stood for a long time staring into the mirror. Green eyes gazed back at her as she revisited every line, wrinkle, curve, and shadow. It was a face she was comfortable with and had grown used to over the years as it had aged and matured. But it was time to let go now, time to move on. She had known it for a while but tried to delay the inevitable for as long as possible.

A single tear trickled down her cheek. Vanessa placed her finger on the mirror and traced the reflection of the tears, following its path as it wended down her once beautiful face.

She took a deep breath and composed herself; now was not the time to indulge her emotions. Now was the time for action. At least she wouldn't have to say goodbye! She had told her friends and neighbours that she was emigrating to New Zealand to live with the boyfriend she had met through an online dating website. The universal response to this was shock and dismay. She had lost count of the times she had been told she was too hasty and rushed into things. It didn't matter. It was only a cover story, anyway. She just needed to disappear from their lives.

Vanessa had told people that Miranda, her niece from London, was moving up to Drumnadrochit. Miranda would be taking over the small shop Vanessa ran, selling ice creams and drinks to the tourists and a plethora of Loch Ness souvenirs and novelty items. Vanessa had run the shop for over 25 years and was continually amazed by the absolute rubbish people visiting the loch would buy.

The day finally came for her to leave. All her clothes were packed into three suitcases, which she loaded into her trusty Land Rover. She added a couple of boxes containing stuff she had meant to give to charity. It would help enhance the appearance of her departure. She said fond farewells to the small group who had come to see her off. A few tears were in evidence, and Vanessa felt the pang of regret she always had at lying to those closest to her. With a final smile and wave, she set off down the narrow lane, the village slowly disappearing in her rearview mirror.

She headed for Inverness, silently praying she wouldn't bump into anyone she knew. Once there, she dropped the suitcases and boxes off at a charity shop and then headed for the used car dealer with whom she had already been in contact. It pained her to relinquish the Land Rover. It had served her so well over the past 25 years, but it couldn't be helped. This was part of the price she just had to pay.

The salesman looked dubious as she looked over the bright yellow Toyota RAV-4.

'Are you sure this is the one you want?' he asked. We do have quite a selection of more...' he stumbled, trying desperately to find the most appropriate word. 'Um, more conservative vehicles. Range Rovers, Hondas, and even a newer Land Rover.'

She gave him a withering look, 'I'm sure they're all very nice, young man, but this is the one I want,' she said, looking at the bright yellow SUV. Horrible, she thought privately, this isn't me at all. But then I won't be me soon, will I? So maybe we are ideally suited. She completed the deal, leaving her Land Rover in part exchange and driving away in the Toyota. She parked some distance from the main shopping centre, not wanting anyone to see her driving this awful new car. She walked, feeling the constricting tightness throughout her whole body, just one of the many signs that had forewarned her of what was to come.

A tedious hour was spent with her solicitor signing various official documents to transfer all of her assets, including her flat and shop, into the name of Miranda De Saragon. With the legalities complete, she set about her final task; a shopping spree for new clothes. Vanessa spent the next couple of hours traipsing from one store to the next, increasing the number of shopping bags she carried with each visit. Several times, she received curious looks from the sales assistants, and one or two of them even hesitantly questioned her choices. Whilst she could still just about fit into a size 12, she was much more comfortable wearing size 14 clothes. However, without exception, her new wardrobe consisted entirely of size 8 or 10 clothes, whose style was targeted predominantly at the 20-something demographic.

Her last visit was to a department store, where she bought herself three new, trendy suitcases and a stylish designer handbag for what she considered an obscene amount of money! Once back at the car, she carefully removed all of the price tags from her new clothes and folded them neatly into the new suitcases. Late that night, she drove back to her flat in the village and parked her new car unobtrusively behind the shop. Although how you could do anything discrete with something that yellow, she didn't know.

Careful to avoid being seen, she made her way to the path running alongside the loch. Loch Ness was almost mirror-like in the still night. Its' inky black surface reflected only the faint moonlight, keeping the secrets of its depths hidden. Familiar steps carried her to a small cove a mile along the path.

A yearning rose within her, forceful and unbidden, and Vanessa knew it was time. Her body was becoming alien to her, no longer her own to control, the wracking pain and stiff, awkward movements the final clues that she must give it up. With great difficulty, she commanded her fingers one last time. She slowly removed all her clothes, folded them neatly, and placed them in a plastic bag. The chill night sent a shiver through her naked body, but she ignored it. She knew from many past experiences that there was much colder to come. She placed the bag within a small crevice in one of the many rocks that abounded the edge of the loch, carefully ensuring that it was out of sight. It would raise many unanswerable questions if her clothes were to be found and recognised.

She looked around one last time, savouring the night, and determinedly stepped into the water. The cold bit her feet and lower legs like a multitude of sharp needles piercing her. She gasped involuntarily and stopped. Her body momentarily refused the commands of her mind. She forced herself to take another step further into the loch, the water rising towards her thighs, keeping pace with the cold that spread through her.

Icy footstep after icy footstep, the naked 55-year-old woman slowly entered the piercing, unwelcoming loch. She could no longer tell if the pain coursing through her body was due to the cold or what was happening to her. She stopped one final time as the dark waters lapped at her chin, almost as if her body had finally realised what she intended and refused to go along with the plan. Despite knowing that filling her lungs with air wouldn't help, Vanessa took a deep breath. Raising both arms before her, she dived under the surface, blackness engulfing her completely. She swam, each stroke taking her further from the shore and deeper under the water. The agony wracking her body increased by the second.

Suddenly, the pain was gone. She no longer felt her lungs burning for oxygen. She could see, and this underwater realm welcomed her home. Once more long, sleek, and slender, her body glided effortlessly through the water. Her skin was such a dark green hue that it was almost black.

Her transformation was complete. Her mind was still her own, her thoughts the same, but her body, which for the past 30 years had been that of an auburn-haired human woman, was now that of an ancient creature. The small head atop a long snake-like neck swung back and forth, scanning the depths of the loch, remembering this watery world.

She was a Sea Dragon, the very last of her kind. And rather than spend the countless centuries of her life in isolation, she had chosen to live amongst humans as one of them. But her human body only lasted a few decades. So she was forced, at the end of each one, to revert to her natural form in order to regenerate. It wouldn't take long. Just a few days was all she needed, and she could resume her human life again. In the meantime, she relished being in her natural form, gliding through the dark waters of the loch.

Just once every generation or so, she would allow someone to catch a glimpse of her reptilian form. After all, she did have a living to make, and her business relied on the regular stream of tourists visiting the loch, ever hopeful of catching a glimpse of the elusive Loch Ness Monster. She smiled inwardly, recalling the sign outside her shop; 'Enter and discover the truth of Loch Ness Monster.' If only the tourists realised who was serving them as they bought their tawdry gifts.

And so, three nights later, a young, beautiful woman emerged naked from the loch, water dripping from her long russet hair, penetrating green eyes scanning the beach carefully. She was alone and quietly headed for the rocky crevice where she had stowed the clothes, all of which were now far too big for her slender frame.

Goodbye, Vanessa, she whispered silently, gazing out over the dark waters one last time. I will miss you. And with that, the newly rejuvenated woman returned to her familiar home, ready to start a new life.

Susan Noon

Susan's writing journey began with a one day Adult Education Short Story Writing course. Immediately hooked, she signed up for the Beginner's Novel Writing Course followed by the Advanced Novel Writing course.

Then came her first Swanwick Writers' Summer School; an incredible, inspirational week, totally addictive.

She has written short stories and, using her experience as an actor and director in amateur dramatics, has written several short scripts which have all been performed at the Swanwick Page 2 Stage event.

Susan has also written the first draft of a cosy-crime novel which she needs to retrieve from a drawer and edit.

The Search

By Susan Noon

'The cellar, it must be in the cellar.' Jane had been searching all morning for the ribboned box. She had thought she knew where it was and had started her search in the attic, looking beneath dust sheets and in old, mouldy cardboard boxes. But all to no avail. She stopped for a cup of coffee – just to clear her head, and tried some visualisation techniques that her life coach had taught her. She spent a very pleasant hour drinking coffee, eating digestive biscuits, visualising herself in each room of the house; changing some of the décor as she moved from place to place. It was no good; the box remained elusive, even to her mind's eye.

Jane resumed her physical search in the spare bedroom. She opened the wardrobe doors and spent a productive hour sorting through her redundant winter clothes. A bag of items for the charity shop resulted, but no box. The space under the spare room bed was also fruitless, reminding her that she really must hoover more often. Never a fan of spiders, she was startled by a particularly large specimen which sent her retreating to the kitchen and another cup of coffee with a couple of chocolate digestives.

Glancing at the clock, she realised that time was getting short and she really must resume her search. Of course, it must be in her bedroom. Jane took a duster with her and managed to search and dust every shelf, cupboard and drawer in the room. Another pleasant half hour spent admiring and cleaning forgotten heirlooms and hand-made treasures, but still no box. Slowly, she walked downstairs. She knew that the box was not in the living room or the conservatory, both rooms had recently been emptied for redecorating and the box had certainly not been evident. So where could it be? She must find it and time was running out.

The cellar, it had to be the cellar. She rarely visited the dark room. It was full of shadows and strange smells, making you constantly look over your shoulder to check if you were alone. She took a large torch and gingerly walked down the creaky wooden stairs into the darkness. There were several large plastic crates in a corner and she flashed her torch in each one, fumbling with pieces of old fabric, books and, at last, a bright pink box with an elaborate bow on it. 'Thank goodness,' she cried, and took the box upstairs.

The doorbell rang. 'Good afternoon great Aunt Patricia. Do come in,' greeted Jane ushering in the formidable lady standing in the doorway.

'Ah, Jane, good to see you and, I am pleased to see you still have my vase gracing your hall table; such a beautiful thing for your visitors to see as they enter.'

'Yes,' replied Jane, wondering where she could hide the vase before her great aunt's next visit.

The Perfect Pet

By Susan Noon

'Oh Jerry,' sighed Gloria. 'It just won't do I'm afraid.'

Jerry picked up the tabby kitten and stroked it absentmindedly.

'What's wrong this time, Gloria? I thought Tiddles would be perfect.'

'Well dear, I can see why <u>you</u> would, but to a creative eye like mine, the aesthetics just aren't right.'

'Oh, shall I take her back then?' asked Jerry, tickling Tiddles under the chin.

'Yes dear and, this time, see if you can find something a little more interesting. The animal has to be a key feature in the whole design, not just blend into the background.'

'Very well,' sighed Jerry, resigned to yet another journey to the pet shop in town. 'What are you going to do while I'm gone? Perhaps you could get some dinner on?'

'Oh darling, I am far too busy to think about preparing meals. It will have to be a microwave treat again tonight. I have to finish painting the cornice, sanding the occasional tables and distressing the oak chair. Not to mention touching up the wallpaper where you lent on it yesterday.'

'Yes of course my dear. I didn't realise it had just been put up.'

'Well, off you go. Farewell Tiddles.' Gloria gave the kitten a disparaging look as she returned to her painting.

Jerry carried Tiddles carefully back to the box in the car. 'Looks like it's the pet shop for you again,' he said gently. 'You are beautiful. I quite fancy the idea of a cat around the house. Unfortunately, you don't fit in with her new interior design project – the Amazon in Dudley Road.'

He drove slowly to the shop where he handed Tiddles back to the owner. 'Not right Jerry?'

'No Sid, she didn't pass Gloria's eagle eye. Apparently she doesn't look right against the jungle fauna mural in the living room.'

'And neither did the Jack Russell or the house rabbit?'

'No, afraid not. I think it might have to be something a bit more exotic this time.'

'I think I've got just what you need, right here in this case. But be careful some people are very allergic to the hairs on their legs – a reaction can be fatal.'

'Well, she wanted exotic and exciting,' Jerry smiled.

Jerry held the case at arm's length as he took it into the house. 'Gloria, how about this chap?' he said as he set the case on the floor and opened the door.

'Ah, much better. He fits the theme perfectly and Mrs Henshaw down the road will be most impressed, he's much more exciting than her guinea pig. Can I stroke him?'

'Err, yes, of course,' said Jerry as the eight black legs slowly clambered onto the chair leg.

***

'Come on Tiddles, time for your tea,' said Jerry to the purring ball of fur on his knee. 'A lovely plate of fish for you, and a juicy steak for me.'

That Colour Suits You

By Susan Noon

John looked in the mirror and grimaced. He definitely looked a bit peaky, pale, a bit green around the gills, as his mother would have said. His boss had commented on it in the office earlier that day, asking him if he'd had a late night. John felt tired, but other than that, quite well, so he decided a hot mug of cocoa and an early night would probably do the trick.

He awoke late the next morning and dashed round his flat getting ready for work, just managing to catch his bus before it consigned him to a late mark. He slumped into his chair, 'Hey John, you alright mate?' asked Robert across the desk.

'Yeah, overslept but I'm fine,' he replied. 'Why?'

'Well, you look… well, a bit out of sorts.'

John began to feel a little concerned, 'What do you mean?'

'You're very pale. Are you feeling cold or shivery?'

'No, I feel fine, had an early night. Perhaps it's the lighting in here.'

'Yeah, maybe,' muttered Robert, sounding unconvinced.

John studied his reflection again that night. He did look pale, but more than that, he looked as though his skin was becoming dull and matt. He looked at his hands; they too seemed to have lost their pinkness. Perhaps he should go to see the doctor – he couldn't remember the last time he had been. No, maybe he could pop into the pharmacists on the way to work in the morning.

John awoke and stretched, made his way into the bathroom and stopped. He stared at the face in the mirror – it was green! A rather soft, muted shade of sage – but it was green. 'How? What the…' he stuttered. He looked down at his hands, his arms and torso – all a delicate shade of green. Going closer to the mirror, he stared at his eyes; not the pale grey ones that usually looked back, but a pair of emerald orbs with deep black pupils.

Green – he was green! He showered, hoping that somehow his colour would change; but clear water ran down the plughole and his skin remained minty. Not knowing what else to do, he got dressed, had breakfast and caught the bus to work. People stared and laughed, obviously thinking this was some sort of prank or fancy dress that had gone wrong.

He walked into the office. 'Blimey!' said Robert looking at his friend. John took his seat and opened his computer with its screensaver displaying 'Chazeldene and Sons Ltd Experimental Colour and Dying Solutions'.

'You're lucky,' said Robert. 'Green suits you!'

Enough

By Susan Noon

I have had enough of queueing, repeating the same actions every day, having the same worries every day. I queue to get into the Work Unit. I queue to get into the Food Unit and I queue to get into the Sleep Unit. Day after day, the same routine, the same people, the same mundane existence.

The Government have told us that it is all for the common good, to create equality. But this equality is meaningless, impersonal, demeaning. Not the sort of equality that allows us all to thrive, and people to raise themselves up, to succeed. This equality is just control of the masses.

As I queue for my place in the Food Unit, I look around me: young people talking, comparing notes on their day's work, even though they have all been doing very similar things. What can I say? The components were all in the correct order, the workstations all sanitised, and the clock on the wall seemed to move slower than ever. My shift finished and I left the Work Unit as another queued to enter.

I sit with two others and we start eating our Day 5, ration D meal. It tastes better than it sounds and, of course, the nutritionists have made sure that it contains everything our bodies need to remain healthy workers. We talk about irrelevant things; the weather and how long it will be before we can become one of the Outsiders in the Pasture. Another four years for me, six for them. I don't think I can do this for another four days, let alone four years.

I leave the Food Unit and look across at the queue for the Sleep Unit. The powder in our food ensures that we sleep well, to keep us fit for working, but I do not feel like sleeping. I feel that I have had enough. I can't do this anymore. I will not wait any longer for my time to go to Pasture, I must go now. I take a deep breath of the ozone filled, recycled air and run. No one comes after me. I run as fast as I can towards the barrier: the barrier between me and the freedom of the Pasture. The jolt is surprisingly pleasurable – a violent tingling surges through my body and I scream as I fall into the sleep of no future.

Enough.

Like Mother, Like Daughter

By Susan Noon

She stood in the middle of the vast bedroom and looked around her. The bed was a king size divan; one tiny part for her, the rest for the mountain of cuddly toys she had amassed. Wardrobes filled one wall, full of beautiful patterns and prints. A door led into a pretty pink bathroom where her shower was decorated with sparkly tiles. This was Skye's kingdom – but she did share it.

'Come on down Skye love. Dinner's ready!' The shout came from the dining room where her family gathered every evening for their meal.

'Don't worry, I'll be back soon,' she whispered as she left the room. Skye ate her dinner with her mum, dad and two elder brothers. The chat was friendly and funny – the boys told stories about their schoolmates and her dad made fun of her mum's cooking. At the end of the meal, Skye announced that she would be going back to her room.

'Are you ok up there sweetie?' asked her mum. 'You know you can come and watch some tele in the living room with me.'

'I'm fine. I like it in my room,' she replied as she danced up the stairs.

'You know, that child spends too much time on her own,' said her father. 'She never brings friends home to play with. Perhaps we should arrange some play dates.'

'Leave her be,' replied her mother. 'I think she's quite content. You know what I've always said; I don't want her mixing too much with the local kids. The boys are ok, they can stick up for themselves, but Skye's like me – she's different.'

‘Ok, ok, as long as she’s happy.’

Skye sat on the floor in her room playing dress up with one of her dolls. She was talking, explaining her reasoning for each outfit. Her eyes glanced repeatedly at a space in the corner. The old lady, who sat there, smiled contentedly watching her. Skye looked up as her mother walked in. ‘I’ve brought you a glass of milk love. Are you ok?’

‘Yes mum. Look, this is my favourite outfit.’

‘That’s lovely,’ she said, sitting on the floor. She smiled over at the old lady and whispered a quiet ‘thank you’. She knew that old Mrs Jenkins would always be watching over her daughter, just as she had watched over her.

One Man's Treasure

By Susan Noon

(A five minute play script written for the Swanwick Page to Stage competition.)

Characters:

JJ – burglar

Lou – burglar

Jim – friend of Bert's

Fred – friend of Bert's

Rachel – Bert's niece (voice heard offstage)

Bert – old gentleman, very poor eyesight, celebrating his birthday

Set:

Bert's living room: sofa, 2 chairs, several small tables

Props:

Toby jug, single cup and saucer, velvet pouch containing coins, old book, small pile of books, photograph frame with photograph of lady, other assorted ornaments, large bag / holdall, bottle of whisky, whisky glasses.

(JJ and Lou enter tentatively)

JJ: Told you, piece of cake. Old sash window, quick jemmy and we're in.

Lou: Yeh, but why here? This place doesn't look anything special.

JJ: I've heard that the old chap who lives here has some nice gear. You know, collector's stuff. My mate 'in the business' *(taps side of nose)* says it'll fetch a pretty penny at auction.

Lou: But how do we get it to an auction if it's nicked?

JJ: Don't you worry about the details – just remember, it's not what you know, it's who. *(Taps side of nose again)*

Lou: Just as long as we get enough to make it worth our while.

JJ: Don't you worry, from what I hear we've landed in the middle of a treasure trove.

Lou: *(Looking around)* Did your mate say exactly what we're looking for? All looks like tatty crap to me.

JJ: One man's tatty crap is another man's treasure Lou, don't you worry, there's plenty here. *(Picks up Toby jug)* Ugly looking chap isn't he, but I reckon he's worth about two hundred and fifty quid. *(Puts jug in large bag)*

Lou: You're kidding. You been watching the Antiques Roadshow?

JJ: Nah, Fiona Bruce – not my type.

Lou: How do you know about all this stuff then?

JJ: Bit of research mate. Some of these collectors are nutters. They'll pay top money for what you and I think of as rubbish.

Lou: More money than sense I reckon.

JJ: Who cares as long as they're giving their money to us?

(JJ and Lou continue looking round)

Nice frame – worth a bit. Ditch the picture, polish it up. Quid's in! *(Puts frame in bag)*

Lou: What about this? *(Holds up a velvet pouch)* Full of coins, looks as though it could be special. *(Puts pouch in bag)*

JJ: Great, rare coins. Collectors go mad for 'em. Never seen the attraction myself but at least they don't take up much room. Don't get in the way of the missus dusting.

Lou: My missus can't stand clutter. She'd kill me if I started leaving this sort of thing lying about. Look at this, just one cup and saucer, what's the point in that? *(Hands cup and saucer to JJ)*

JJ: It must be Royal Doulton or Wedgewhere or something special. Very dainty. *(Demonstrates drinking with little finger sticking out, puts cup and saucer in the bag)*

Lou: There's a pile of books over here. This one looks old.

JJ: Great, put it in the bag. A nice first edition, we'll be rolling in it. *(Lou puts book in bag)*

(Clatter off stage)

Lou: Hey, did you hear that? There's someone coming.

JJ: Nah, he's out at some birthday bash from what I heard.

(More clatter offstage)

Lou: Well it sounds like he's come back early.

JJ: Don't panic, come here behind the sofa and we'll wait for our chance to skip out. He's an old bloke, bad eyesight, can't move very fast. *(JJ and Lou duck down behind sofa. Jim and Fred enter. Jim carries a whisky bottle and has obviously already had a drink.)*

Jim: Come on, we haven't got long before he gets back.

Fred: Are you sure he doesn't know we're gonna be here?

Jim: Has no idea. Gone out to dinner with his niece, thinks we're all otherwise engaged for the evening. Didn't think we could let his birthday go by without a bit of a celebration.

Fred: Poor sod'll have a heart attack if we're not careful.

Jim: Don't you underestimate our Bert. I know he's as blind as a ferret in an undertaker's trousers but there's nothing wrong with his hearing. He'll probably know we're here before we get the chance to shout 'Surprise!'

Fred: *(Moves across room behind sofa)* Hello – what do we have here?

(JJ and Lou stand up)

JJ: Er, great. A party. We had the same idea, thought we'd catch him by surprise.

Lou: Er, yeh. That's right. Heard you coming and thought it was him.

Jim: Well, the more the merrier.

(Clatter offstage)

Fred: Shh, here he comes.

(All crouch behind furniture)

Bert: *(Offstage)* Thank you Rachel, that was a lovely meal. So kind of you to treat an old man on his birthday.

Rachel: *(Offstage)* No problem Uncle Bert, I always enjoy an evening with you. I'll be off now, enjoy the rest of your day, see you next Monday.

Bert: *(Offstage)* Bye love, thanks again.

(Bert enters. Jim and Fred stand up)

Jim / Fred: Surprise!

(Lou and JJ stand up and look at each other shrugging their shoulders)

Lou / JJ: Yeh, surprise!

Bert: Oh my goodness, how wonderful! What a birthday! *(Bert sits on sofa)* Now, who's here?

Jim: Come off it Bert, I know the old eyesight isn't up to much but we know you can hear a pin drop at a hundred yards and tell us what it was made of.

Bert: *(Laughing)* You got me there Jim. It sounds as though you've had a couple of celebratory drinks already.

Jim: Told you, nothing gets past him.

Bert: Who else have we got then?

JJ: Oh, er, hello Bert. It's JJ and Lou. You remember us?

Bert: *(Pauses)* Oh… yes… of course.

Jim: Fred's here too. He hasn't heard about your treasures yet – come on let's have your party piece.

Bert: Oh, I'm sure you don't want to hear about my little knick-knacks.

Fred: I reckon a birthday is the perfect time for a little trip down memory lane.

Bert: *(Obviously pleased)* Oh alright, if you insist. Now what shall we start with?

Jim: Got to be the jug.

Bert: *(Laughing)* Ok, pass it over.

(JJ and Lou look at each other panic stricken. Unseen by the others, JJ reaches into the bag and passes the Toby jug forward to Bert)

JJ: Is this it? Here you go.

Bert: Er… thank you. *(Running his hands over the Toby jug)* This lovely old fella was given to me by Monsieur Picardy on the 10th June 1944. I was in a battalion moving north after landing on Sword beach on D Day. He owned a hostelry in the village of Armand where we camped for the night. I remember the look in his eye as he pressed old Toby into my hands. Couldn't understand much of what he was saying, but his eyes – the relief. Toby was his way of saying thank you to a Tommy who was helping to save his country. I carried him all the way home in my pack and not a single crack or chip. I only hope Monsieur Picardy survived in as good a condition.

Jim: That jug is incredibly ugly but that story, that is beautiful.

Bert: Now if you want beauty you want the photo of Lily. Pass the frame can you?

(Unseen by the others Lou looks furtively in the bag and passes the frame)

(Running hands over frame) Ah, here she is. Lily Watts, the love of my life. Bless her. Do you know it's 12 years since she's been gone?

Fred: Is it that long?

Bert: In some ways it feels like only weeks but in others it feels like a lifetime. This is the last picture she had taken. I can't see it properly now but I just have to hold this frame and I can see it up here *(taps head)*. She had a pale blue dress on which matched the colour of her eyes and she was standing next to the pink rosebush in the garden – still flowers you know. Her smile could outshine the brightest star.

(Pause)

Fred: What else have you got Bert?

Bert: Pass me the velvet pouch. It's over there *(pointing to a small table)*.

JJ: *(Quickly getting the pouch out of the bag)* I've got it, here you go.

Bert: The two proudest days of my life – the day I married my Lily and the day I was given this. I was given the Maundy Money at Winchester Cathedral by her Majesty herself. She handed me this pouch, her white glove touched my hand and she looked straight into my eyes and smiled. Our Queen… smiling at me!

Fred: Didn't know we were in such esteemed company.

Jim: Oh Bert, you always manage to bring a tear to my eye.

Bert: Oh get on with you, me and my knick-knacks?

Jim: I think it's time for a drink. You got any glasses?

Bert: In the kitchen. There are some biscuits in the cupboard too.

(Jim and Fred exit to kitchen)

Bert: Er, JJ and Lou was it?

(JJ and Lou move towards the front door)

JJ: Erm, yes, that's right. We ought to be off. Enjoy the rest of your birthday.

Bert: Just a minute, haven't you forgotten something?

Lou: Have we?

Bert: I'll have my Royal Doulton.

JJ: Oh the cup and saucer. Yeh, well, sorry Bert. *(Takes cup and saucer out of the bag and hands them to Bert)*

Bert: And the book. *(Takes book from JJ)* Thank you gents, can't let <u>them</u> go. Souvenirs from when I had tea at the Ritz.

Lou: I expect you were having tea with some Maharajah or something.

Bert: It was John Le Carré actually. Said he would put me in one of his stories, lovely fella.

Lou: Really?

Bert: Oh yeh, <u>great storyteller</u>. *(Gives a big wink and a knowing smile)* I keep them here, safe with all my other treasures. Goodnight gentlemen.

(JJ and Lou exit)

Liam Thompson

Liam lives in the small coastal town of Skerries, on the outskirts of Dublin city. He writes predominantly poetry, though he occasionally turns his hand to children's stories in between, for good measure.

His poems are generally reflections on ordinary everyday observations that strike a cord within, which meander by times into a semi spiritual or philosophical space.

He has been published in various Irish poetry journals and magazines. He hopes to devote more time and effort to the pleasure of writing, and the business of it.

Kennelly

By Liam Thompson

I see you standing Brendan; you're on a stage,
Smiling at the lady who's just sneezed.
And almost saint like from mischievous eyes
You look softly south, swapping spectacles

For a second pair you slip from your coat;
One you say is for long distances,
And the other for looking at beautiful girls.
We laugh as I picture your wisp and your curl,

Click the cut of you - make mental images
Of a man whom everyman could love;
A surrogate for a lover gone,
For a brother lost, a late father, or a son.

You speak and we ooh and we ahh and we coo
Over how you hold us, with the words you mould
Into a slow, unhurried, gentle dreamy dance -
Where you turn and twirl us to entrance.

We are Sufi spinning to the sacred rhythm

Of your rhyme, then you waltz us slower, three four time;

Outward by the blue rinsed ladies and the belle,

Along the inner city streets, by tall Parnell;

We dance to Ballylongford, to Kavanagh's canal

And after Smithfield we resume our seats and swoon

Beside a woman with the wounded wrists; like her we're cut

But ours concealed - inside the heart, within the fist.

The Last Curlews

By Liam Thompson

I saw the last curlews set off from Skerries strand,
A silhouette of three, one Sunday at sunset.
Their thin legs skittered them seawards over the sands
As if they were in a hurry somewhere,
Like migrants leaving a land where they were
No longer welcome, humbled or embittered
At being here, better now to be gone
And not wanting to be seen as they went.
Nice to dream that they felt the imminence of a new flood
And left for the sanctuary of some mystical isle,
Or a mythical ark, anchored invisibly offshore.
And while there will be time, even in gravest times to turn,
I fear tomorrows newly born, walking as adults
On this same strand, seeing it almost emptied of its sacred life
And saying of us who've gone, 'Jesus! They've left us nothing!'

Taking the Foal

By Liam Thompson

All night long the mare
has whinnied at the gate.
Though dark, I could see
her silhouette turn about
and trample the soft turf.
Just yesterday, the horsebox
was hauled into the field,
where men in boots and caps
and black waxed jackets,
clapped and whooped;
waved their arms wide
till soon they severed
foal from dam; corralled
them, tethered the colt.
Minutes later it was gone;
and its days stood shy
and contented by the side
of its mothers hind legs,
or nuzzled in, eyes blinking
to a slow close and some equine
dream, had suddenly dashed.

Swallows

By Liam Thompson

It's late September, and the last
swallows still circle round the roofs.
Perhaps there was a late brood to be fed
before the faraway journey begins.
But it's grey; the low cloud seems to capture
a sense of heavy heartedness that holds me.
These last days, death has come so early
for some - far too beautiful, far too young.
A young boy who by his own hands has gone
beyond the clutches of these cold climes;
and a girl who has fed upon the pickings of
a meagre summer plate and has followed on.
But I have some sense of their sadness
when their urge to go was just too great;
unlike these swallows leaving late, instead they've
sought the south, its sun - but way too soon.

Pelican in a Slick

By Liam Thompson

She is a silhouette, stuck beneath the
High sun on the sea off the Deep South.
Her dark shape backlit against a bright
Blue sky is bobbing, her eyes throbbing
Blearily, weary and barely able to breathe.
Her nostrils clogged, every crevice closed,
She is bogged down and covered with crude oil.
One fisherman curses his fate; infuriates
Over the fools that foisted this on him,
'They gotta fix this; I ain't done nuthin' wrong,
He says, as the poison continues to pour and
The Pelican makes a vain attempt to fly free,
Collapses to a smother of dense brown sludge,
Where even from this distance I feel stained.
Yet for all our lessons there is little to show we learn,
And no sense of a true salvation from our sins.
Save perhaps our oil stained souls are sluiced,
Sieved clean, and strained through the eye of a needle.

St. Francis and the Siren

By Liam Thompson

Had your eyes intended anything they said,
I could have fallen backwards into love.
Became a troubadour again; my life spent serenading
Your embodiment of every other woman in the world.
So when I had to leave and knew departure
Came too soon to let your lyric take my hand,
I imagined us instead as secret lovers at a cross,
You all teary eyed and trembling in my arms;
Within my sight the whitest stallion saddled up in wait.
But knowing even then, the journey I would choose,
My leaving you behind, would set within my soul
An empty space that evermore without you would remain
Remote and incomplete, sorrowful, eternally calling.

The Sculptress Considers her Art

By Liam Thompson

From the very centre of myself I feel a surge,
That travels, tingling, mingling with bone
And blood, flooding forward through my hands.
And this stone I touch has taken aeons to emerge,
And my thoughts the same; and their facade is
The surface and the texture of the depths I dig;
Layer upon layer of words, wants, abundance, acts,
The silt and sedimentary facts, becomes firm
And begets the form which promises to show;
Revealed this time in the rough shape of a heart,
Thumping from the spirit of a child, it is woken
Having broken from the mould, and beating hard.
I will bear every shape I make like a baby born,
Both midwife and mother after a beautiful birth,
The child asleep at my bare breast, awhile at one
With something of myself, before I place her
Swaddled in the very fabrics of my soul and set
Her in a basket of reed, and sail her upstream;
Abandoned to the burden of the bearers eye, to call
Her beauty as an abstract truth or an absolute lie.

Foghorns

By Liam Thompson

'Here's the big boat coming in'
he'd say before he'd blow across
the mouth of an empty milk bottle.
Then a low, resonant, siren like
sound would sail the short distance
over the wet cobbles and the roofs;
across railway carriages and 1960's cars,
the Seville Place bridge and the Five Lamps,
from the fogbound Dublin city docks.

My father has lulled me to a light sleep
and left; I can hear the kettle and the cups
as he sets the table out for supper.
The window is rattled by the wind;
the curtain billows from a broken pane.
But all the ships are in safe now;
I can see their funnels tucked up tight
to the Liffey walls; the Mail boat,
the Manx ferry, Miranda Guinness.

Como

By Liam Thompson

Lake Como's light breeze is cooling
the long day at last. And will it be
stood there, looking back from the stern
of 'Senza Timore' that I'll learn to live
once more without mere words?
Out here, for all their talk of love,
these sailors say little that's not dressed
first for style, the substance might just
take a while to come, or not arrive.
On the far sided shore in Dongo,
I heard Il Duce had his final say;
'Shoot me in the chest!' he said,
and they obliged, and too his lover laid beside.
I set my arms out wide in the same way
and was struck, slightly centre left,
and have struggled ever since to stand.
But maybe what I need to steady up
is soundless, unsettled and unsure?
It's the shape of a shrug at an ill-boding sea,
it's the grand talk let go, and the tiller.

After June

By Liam Thompson

As I sit here, a low mist
forms over the downs;
makes the hills seem grey
above the lush green grass

as each day sees the scene
change at the weather's call.
There is no reason that
I should not write you.

Today I took the dog walking
over autumns fresh fields and
returned with a new verse;
perhaps this will be the final

one that I send you.
Last night I watched the rim
of the moon push through
a break in the backlit clouds,

and from a space behind me I
heard a voice, 'put that in a poem',
you told me, 'call it Illuminate'.
For you always knew things;

when the first swallow would
swoop in from the south,
where the lark would land in
the long grass after her great ascent.

You said too, you knew so much
of me; so therefore tell me this!
Why the breeze played a slow air
down the length of the long lane

by which you took your leave,
and why the songbirds fell silent
as this sad song swelled my heart,
And why are you so far away?

Tomorrow I may take the train
from the town, out toward the cliffs
where we fell in love last June;
and with me take the leaving
of our final days and fling them

furthest from me that I can -
the silence and the slamming doors,
your fading figure disappear,

the stillness of that empty room.
Oh love, my mind is burdened
and my face buried into the
crook of the arm that you once caught;

it will not rise again till you return.
I am a lone swan adrift on a lake
I am a half writ word, a wasted pen,

I am the last Unicorn

Thoughts to leave you with …

Timed Writes

Creativity is a muscle, it needs exercising regularly to grow and develop. One technique that some of us have found useful is timed writing.

There are numerous books & websites which provide writing prompts. Set a timer, find your prompt, and without any further thought or planning, write. Yes, just write.

Entering Competitions

Entering competitions is a great way to flex your creativity muscle, and practice writing to a deadline. You'll find them in such places as magazines, websites and events.

Using AI

Artificial Intelligence is a great help, but its artificial nature is easy to spot. It is best used for research and inspiration. A human mind is better at the creativity.

The Search for Perfection

Perfection is rare and nebulous, and like beauty, maybe only be true for the beholder. This is especially true of creative perfection. Therefore do not let the search for the perfect opening line prevent you from writing the rest of the story. Listen to your editors, your beta readers and accept 'good enough'.

Find your Tribe

Writing can be lonely. Find a group of like-minded people you can trust. Sharing ideas, work in progress and finished tomes is immeasurably beneficial.

Why not try Swanwick

We all met at Swanwick. We found our tribe. You might find yours there too, or if you don't you're sure to have a hugely inspirational week.

Swanwick

THE

writers'

SUMMER SCHOOL

swanwickwritersschool.org.uk

Printed in Dunstable, United Kingdom

66280965R00088